GUNSLINGERS THREE

Chet King, respected as a man, but feared for the mercilessness of his angry guns, rode out from obscurity into the blazing fury of a border feud. King was a Westerner, living and dying by the West's law. This is the story of his stand for the justice which was all he really believed in.

GORDON D. SHIRREFFS

GUNSLINGERS THREE

Complete and Unabridged

LINFORD
Leicester

First Linford Edition
published April 1989

British Library CIP Data

Shirreffs, Gordon D. (Gordon Donald)
    Gunslingers three.—Large print ed.—
Linford western library
I. Title
813′.54[F]

    ISBN 0-7089-6682-9

Published by
F. A. Thorpe (Publishing) Ltd.
Anstey, Leicestershire
Set by Rowland Phototypesetting Ltd.
Bury St. Edmunds, Suffolk
Printed and bound in Great Britain by
T. J. Press (Padstow) Ltd., Padstow, Cornwall

1

THEY had splashed across the shallow waters of the Rio Grande from Chihuahua at dusk, a spit and a holler ahead of the Guardia Rurale, with bullets whistling through the velvety darkness and the Mexican shore blossomed with gun flashes. By dawn of the next day they were slanting across the very western tip of Texas, carefully avoiding El Paso, *and* the keen-eyed gentlemen of the Frontier Battalion, Texas Rangers. By dusk of that day they had reached Hueco Tanks on the old Butterfield Trail, with two of them riding double and the third member of the hard riding trio now afoot, leading his exhausted bayo coyote gelding.

Chet King turned in his saddle and grinned at Jimmy Carson, riding double with him. "Told you we'd make it, Kid," he said in a thirst cracked voice.

"You made it alone," said Jimmy. "You left my dried out carcass back there somewheres. This is only my spirit riding with you, Chet."

The big man afoot wrinkled up his magnificent bent nose. "By Jesus!" he said, "I didn't think a ghost could smell that bad."

"You ain't exactly a lily, Bung," said the Kid.

Chet slid from the saddle and eased his aching crotch. "Getting too old for rides like that anymore," he said quietly in his soft voice. He pulled his Winchester from the saddle scabbard and levered a round into the chamber. He eyed the brooding hulk of Hueco Tanks and the conical peak of Cerro Alto rising sharp against the dark sky, marking the eastern entrance to Hueco Pass. They were still in Texas, a handful of miles from the New Mexico line, but they needed the water held in the natural tanks that had been eroded by time and weather in the soft granite.

"Yuh sure they's water in there?" said Bung Burkbennett doubtfully.

"Always has been," said Chet. "Stay here." He vanished into the chapparral like a lean ghost.

"Beats me how he can disappear like that," said Bung. "Just like he was an Apache."

Jimmy dismounted and leaned against the saddle. "I'm dying for a smoke," he said. He raised his head. There was no sound other than the dry voice of the West Texas wind amidst the greasewood and ocotillo that stippled the harsh, sterile earth. "He's got Indian blood in him, Bung."

"He never told me *that!*"

The Kid shrugged. "Never told me either. He didn't have to."

"Don't never let him hear you say he's a breed."

The Kid turned a little and his innocent looking blue eyes studied Bung. "I don't think he'd care, Bung. Matter of fact, I think he's a little *proud* of it, amigo."

The wind shifted a point. It carried the soft sound of a whistle to the two waiting men. They led the two worn out horses towards the humped shapes of the giant clutter of rocks that enclosed the tanks. The area was big, nearly a mile long and half as wide.

"The place is deserted," said Chet from the darkness.

Bung moved a little. It always bothered him to have Chet move about unseen like that even if it was a definite asset in their business. The business of cashing in Colts for silver eagles and folding green.

"What about the stage station?" asked Jimmy.

"Dark," said Chet. "No horses or mules." He grinned. "I figured we might *loan* a couple of mounts from the swing station."

"How come it's deserted?" asked Bung suspiciously.

Chet shrugged. "One of two reasons, Bungo: Either the stage line has gone out of business, which isn't likely, or the Mescaleroes are raiding around here again."

Bung eyed the brooding darkness that shrouded the rocks. "You sure they ain't any of them in there?"

Chet nodded.

Bung didn't argue. If Chet said they weren't in there, they just weren't there. It was as simple as that. They led the horses through a winding labyrinth to the water tanks.

Chet King wasn't as calm as he looked. Twice that afternoon he had seen thin dust wraiths sweeping across the desert. More likely dust raised by hoofs than by the wind. Twice he had seen fresh horse droppings and when he had poked them apart with a stick he had been pretty sure from the food they had eaten that they were more likely from Indian horses than

4

from white men's mounts. East of them was Signal Peak and Guadalupe Pass, and beyond them, to the north, was the haunt of the Mescalero Apaches. Not a long ride for raiders.

Chet squatted on his heels and rolled a cigarette. He grinned as the Kid casually took the finished product from Chet's long fingers and lighted it. "How long do we stay here, Chet?" asked the Kid.

"The horses need rest."

Bung turned from where he lay flat on his belly beside one of the tanks. He wiped his wet mouth. "We got to get out of here before dawn," he said.

"On foot?" said Chet. He rolled another cigarette.

The Kid blew out a ring of smoke. "Too damned hot," he said. He looked at Chet. "Which way we going anyways?"

Chet lighted up and the flare of the match revealed his lean hatchet face and the grey eyes that would startle a man if he wasn't used to them against the mahogany hue of the skin. "Can't go south," he said. "Rangers and Guardia Rurale. Can't go east. More Rangers. West is El Paso and a full company of the Frontier Battalion, Texas Rangers."

"*And* the El Paso police," said Bung. He grinned. "They'll remember us all right." He deftly caught the sack of makings flung to him by Chet.

"That leaves the Territory of New Mexico," said the Kid sonorously. He laughed. "Any of us wanted up there?"

"Not me!" said Bung virtuously.

Chet shook his head.

The Kid blew another ring of smoke. "It's a long way to go," he said.

"Ain't no other way," said Bung. He lighted up.

Chet stood up. He raised his head. "Put out those smokes," he said quietly. He snubbed out his own cigarette and placed the remains in his pocket. "Don't leave them lying around. Take the horses into the rocks over there, Bung. Kid, you wipe out the tracks."

They didn't say a word as they obeyed him. There was an impelling urgency in his voice, behind the softness of it. Then he was gone leaving no trace behind him but the faint drifting odour of tobacco smoke.

Bung led the horses deep into the rock labyrinth, then took his Winchester and loaded the chamber. He was joined by the Kid when

Jimmy had finished wiping out the tracks. The place was quiet except for the soft whispering of the wind and the occasional scuttling of a night creature. An owl drifted overhead on silent, velvety wings.

"Don't breathe so damned hard, Bungo," said the Kid.

"You scairt?"

The Kid shrugged. "I don't mind Yankee lawmen or greaser Rurales," he said. "Indians give me the cold horrors."

"Me too," said the big man. His eyes were hard in his square face. His huge hands tightened on his rifle. "Kill 'em like rats! Vermin!"

Chet appeared as silently as he had vanished. "Horsemen east of here," he said. He didn't have to specify who they were. His two companions knew.

"So?" said the Kid.

"We wait," said Chet.

"Why?" demanded Bung.

"We need horses; they got horses," said Chet simply. He squatted and took out a plug of Winesap and cut a chew which he stowed in his mouth. "Have a chaw," he said. "Liable to be a long wait, amigos."

7

From then on, as the pale moonlight crept across the desert after topping the distant Delawares and tinting the saffron tip of Signal Peak, there was no sound from the trio except the steady movement of jaws and the occasional splattering of the tasty juice as it hit a rounded rock that had been somehow chosen by mutual, though silent consent as the target.

The moon was fully up, bathing the Huecos in cold, silver light when Chet moved out to scout. The tanks were still deserted. There was no sound or light from the stage station. He lay for a long time in a granite saucer shaped hollow high in the middle of the Tanks studying the silent landscape until his eyes picked out movement here and there. Hatless men. The only hatless men in that country weren't white men. The Mescaleroes were surrounding Hueco Tanks as silently as cats.

Chet shifted his chew. The granite was warm under his lean belly, still heated by the rays of the burning West Texas sun. The coming day would be a heller. The two horses, one of them carrying double, would hardly make it to the Sacramentos across the Hueco Desert. What puzzled him was the fact that the Mescaleroes hadn't nailed them at dusk as they entered the

8

tank area. Chet rubbed his lean jaws. He looked west and then east. Maybe they were expecting bigger game, if they knew the three outlaws were hidden amidst the profusion of granite boulders. Big enough game to leave the three white men alone, until such time as they wanted them. They wouldn't likely rush the tanks in the face of repeating rifle fire, nor would they fight at night for fear of being killed, to wander forever in darkness this side of the Spirit Waters.

Somehow he knew when the ring was complete. They made no effort to approach the tanks. Chet worked his way down to his two companions. They hid the horses separately, filled their canteens, took rifles and what little food they had, and found a natural fortress high amidst the rocks, covering the nearest tank of water, as well as the road that passed north of the tanks, past the empty stage station.

The moon sank down in the west while Bung and Chet slept. It was dark when Bung awoke Chet for the last watch, the dangerous one; the pre-dawn watch. Dawn favoured Apache attack. They were guerilla fighters; tip and run. Move in and kill when the enemy is drugged with

9

sleep and his morale is at the lowest. Never give him a chance.

There was the faintest suspicion of dawn light in the eastern sky when Chet heard the muffled sound of hoofs and wheels approaching the tanks from the east. He bellied close to the lip of the circle of rocks and peered out along the Butterfield Trail. Something was moving out there. White men. Moving slowly and cautiously. Not too many of them. Moving right into a silent trap of death with a painted face.

Chet roused his companions. They were safe enough; for a time at least. Bigger game was afoot. Maybe somehow in the forthcoming hassle to the death there might be a few stray horses.

The Kid whistled softly as he listened to the sounds approaching the dark tanks. "Jesusita," he said. "They walking right into it, Chet."

"Maybe you want to warn them?" said Bung coldly.

"Don't hardly seem fair not to," said the Kid.

Bung shifted a little and his agate eyes held the Kid's steady gaze. "You got any ideas of being a hero, Kid, and you're on your own!"

"You giving the orders, Bungo?"

The wind shifted. Chet raised his head. Something dark flitted across the dim track of the road and vanished into the rustling brush. "You keep on jawing like that," he said harshly over his shoulder, "and you'll have them picking us out of these rocks like a frog Frenchman picks a snail out'a its shell with a needle. Shut up!"

"I'll warn 'em if I feel like it," said the Kid stubbornly.

Bung spat. "I'm warning *you*," he said thinly.

"Chet?" said the Kid. "What do *you* think?"

There was a long silence.

"Chet?"

There was no movement from Chet King. "We need horses," he said softly. "No more and no less. White men's horses or Mescaleroes' horses. You got any better ideas?"

The light was paler in the east. Something dark moved along the road. A stagecoach. A sure enough Abbott-Downing swaying easily on its great leather thorough-braces, dripping sand from its wheels, hubs chuckling greasily and sand boxes clucking drily in counter melody to the thudding of the team's twenty-four hoofs striking the road. Two men rode the box. Four other men rode as outriders. Soldiers. Yankee soldiers, thought Chet King. He spat to one side. The bluecoated vermin infested Texas from Nacogdoches to El Paso and from the Red River to the Rio Grande. Chet still thought of himself as a Texan, though of Mississippi birth, but he had been in Texas as a welcome guest since '65. Like many unconverted rebels, he took Texas with him wherever he might be, but he couldn't live there in peace.

The dawn light gave enough illumination to see the coach, team and outriders clearly, while the ambushers lay flat against the hard earth. The rush came swiftly and noiselessly. The first arrow drove through the cold dawn air and struck the shotgun messenger in the throat. The second arrow hit the driver in the forehead, killing him instantly, though his gloved hands still had the ribbons threaded through them and his foot still rode the brake. The team bolted at the smell of Apaches and fresh blood. Two hard riding bucks came out of nowhere and headed off the frantic leaders. The dark floor of the desert seemed to sprout more of them. Thick maned, stocky men who moved like hunting cats, with rifles and knives for fangs. A soldier died with a thrown knife between his blue clad shoulder blades. Another went down with his skull crushed by a stone, encased in shrunken rawhide and swung full arm at the end of a pliant handle. Not a shot had been fired.

The first shot was fired. Into the blue. The rookie flipped open the smoking breech of his carbine to reload it. The second shot was fired from pointblank range. A ten gauge shotgun loaded with anything the buck happened to fancy, nails, pebbles, glass and so on. It destroyed the face of the rookie. As he fell from his McClellan his skull was smashed before he hit the ground and his carbine and Colt were stripped from him in a matter of seconds.

The last soldier was an officer. Somewhere they had taught him to be a man. They had *not* taught him how to fight Apaches. His sabre was ripped from its scabbard with a slithering of naked steel and his Colt was drawn crossarm and fired with the left hand. He rode full spur into a knot of the bucks who scattered like windblown chaff while his slugs whined off into space and his sabre cut air. He turned his rearing, plunging chestnut and rode at them again, young face set and white in the greying light. His Colt ran dry with never a hit. His

13

sabre was lagging as the buck rode silently up behind him and neatly skewered him with a lance tipped by two feet of Spanish steel, carrying him from the saddle. His legs kicked spasmodically. His sabre clanged to the ground. His mouth squared and spewed blood in a thick mist. Then he was face down on the ground while keen edged knives stripped his uniform from his weakly thrashing body. He was rolled over and one swipe of a curved knife made a capon of him and he died with that shameful knowledge the last thing in his frightened mind.

The bucks gathered near the coach. Some of them led the captured horses of the soldiers. Others quietened the frightened team. The dawn light revealed the broad, impassive faces, streaked white with bottom clay; the thick manes of hair bound by dingy headcloths; the basilisk eyes and the thin slits of mouths. A horse whinnied. A bloodstained hand ripped open a door of the coach. A gun exploded from within the coach. The buck at the door staggered back, clutching his naked left shoulder. Gun smoke swirled out of the dark interior of the coach. Two bucks opened the other door and vanished inside the coach.

"Jesusita," said Jimmy Carson. He closed his eyes.

A woman screamed and tore the silence from the dawning desert. Her scream was echoed by another scream. Two women! They were hauled from the coach and hard hands ripped at their travelling clothes. Cold pale light shone on naked breasts and smooth white shoulders. One of them was young and blonde and she screamed almost insanely as she was thrown to the hard ground. The other fought like a man, silently and desperately, her unbound dark hair cascading in sharp contrast against the ivory whiteness of her nakedness. Then she too was down on the ground and a buck stood over her, still impassively, ignoring the weakening beating of her small fists against his desert moccasins. One of the younger bucks laughed.

"Jesusita," said the Kid again. He reached for his rifle.

A hard hand clamped down on the rifle and the Kid looked into Chet King's icy grey eyes. "They don't know we are here, Kid," he said.

"Yeh," said Bung. "*We're* safe anyways."

The blonde woman screamed thinly as greasy hands pawed at her. Her soft skin was being abraded by the harsh caliche soil upon which

15

she lay helplessly, waiting for ravishment. There were a baker's dozen of the bucks. Thirteen of them. Each would take his turn and the pitiful remains would be finished off. She was hardly more than eighteen years old.

"For God's sake, Chet!" said the Kid.

"We need horses, nothing more," said Bung uncertainly.

Chet picked up his rifle. "Looks like we get 'em the hard way," he said. "Come on, amigos! *Andele!*" He vanished down the rocky slope like a gecko lizard.

2

THREE brass-bellied Winchester .44/40's fired as one from the shelter of a rock ledge and three Mescaleros went down like pipe targets in a shooting gallery. Before the startled bucks could move three more of them had hit the dirt. One of them had been wounded. He drew his knife from the top of his moccasins and wormed his way towards the two screaming women. There was no way to get a clear shot at him. Chet King vaulted the rock ledge and ran forward through the swirling mingled dust and powdersmoke, under covering fire of his two companions.

The Apaches began to return fire. Bung Burkbennett cursed savagely as a slug creased his left shoulder. His smoking rifle clattered to the ground. The Kid dropped a retreating warrior, and then his rifle jammed. He dropped it and slid over the rock face, drawing twin Colts as he did so. He walked forward through the smoke firing alternately with the sixguns.

Chet fired once and the slug bored the

Apache through the chest just as his knife missed the dark haired girl by inches. Horses thudded past. Chet reached out and gripped the bridle reins of one of them holding the rearing, plunging beast between him and the shrieking Apaches.

The Kid was in his glory, sowing hot lead like a Kansas sodbuster sowing spring wheat. His hat was whipped off by a slug revealing his wavy blond hair. Another slug flickered his right bicep just as his left Colt went dry. He did the border shift and dropped one of the last of the Mescaleroes in the perfect timing of a top gun.

Then suddenly it was all over as quickly as it had started. Four of the bucks were vanishing into the desert. Two more thrashed about on the ground. The rest had departed for The House of Spirits.

Chet garnered four more excited horses. The Kid reloaded and ran to the coach, ripping several blankets from the interior. He kept his face averted as he walked towards the two silent girls, now sitting up and clutching their torn clothing against their bodies. Bung Burkbennett was still cursing as he ripped his shirt and undershirt from his shoulder to staunch the flowing of blood. Then his hard eyes saw the two thrashing bucks. He heaved himself to his feet and walked steadily towards the two warriors. They lay still as he approached, watching him with glittering eyes. His two gun shots seemed almost like one. The younger woman screamed, then fainted. The dark haired woman covered her with a blanket and then stood up, draping the second blanket about her body and long, lovely legs. She swept back her dark hair with a free hand and looked at Chet King as he reloaded his weapons.

Chet grounded his Winchester. "Are you all right, ma'am?" he asked.

She smiled faintly. "Cut up a little here and there," she said. She blushed at the implication. The hard ground must have played fair hell with her tender back skin.

"Is she all right?" said Chet. He jerked a thumb at the blonde.

"Frightened half to death," she said, "but then she was always afraid of the Apaches."

"Who isn't?" he said drily. "You have other clothing?"

"In the rear boot. The two smaller valises, Mister . . ." She paused and looked at him expectantly.

"Just call me Chet," he said quickly. He led four of the horses towards the natural entrance to the water tanks.

Bung followed Chet. "What now?" he said.

"We can't leave 'em here," said Chet.

"No. But, on the other hand, if the Army finds out it lost some of its boys out here it won't be long before they'll have a detachment of Yankees out here, Chet. They ain't forgot us either, Chet."

Chet smiled a little. "Seems like no one has forgot us, Bungo."

The Kid followed them and examined the horses. "Not bad," he said.

Bung traced the brand US on two of the mounts' dusty hides. "I ain't riding any of *these* babies," he said. "First on account of principle, and second because I don't want them Yankees accusing me of stealing government property."

The Kid grinned. "I'll change them for two of them stage horses," he said. "OK, Chet?"

Chet shrugged. "Then we'll have The Southern Overland looking for us. We haven't been in trouble with them . . . *yet*."

"They might as well join the others," said the big man.

"Look," said the Kid quickly.

They turned to see the two young women walking towards them, the tall dark one supporting the younger blonde one. Bung whistled softly. Both of them were goodlooking, though the taller one was more handsome than downright pretty as was the younger one. The two of them stopped at the edge of the water tank. "I'm Theresa Case," said the darkhaired woman, "and this is my cousin Sarah Case. We want to thank you for saving us."

Chet took off his hat. "These two hombres are Bung and the Kid."

"Thanks," she said. "Bung, the Kid, and Chet. Have you no other names?"

Bung grinned. "Not for publication ma'am," he said.

Her eyes narrowed. "You've been hurt," she said.

"Ain't nothing much," said the big man.

"Nope," said the Kid solemnly. "Ol' Bung here, he wears bullet holes like other men wear jewellery. I mind one time in Tamaulipas when Ol' Bung here . . ." His voice trailed off as he saw the look in the big man's eyes.

She came to Bung and examined the wound. "Have you any medical supplies?"

"They're back in Corps Train," said Chet.

21

"We haven't seen the quartermaster boys for quite awhile this campaign."

"You talk like a soldier," she said.

"The best," said the Kid. "Just ask him." Once again he cut off his banter as Chet shot a glance at him.

"We got a bottle of Abyssinian Desert Companion," said Bung. "Good for wind colic, flatulent colic, botts, diarrhoea, scouring, dysentery, inflammation of the bladder and kidney trouble, colds in the head, congestion, fits, mad staggers, looseness of the bowels, inflammation of the brain, and for botts it has no equal."

Theresa threw back her head and laughed, and the music of it echoed amongst the rocks. Chet King looked more closely at her and a piece of something, long missing from his soul, seemed to slip into place in the void, but there was still a lot of emptiness in that void.

"Used to sell the stuff," said Bung. He grinned. "If it didn't do any other good you could always mix it with lousy whisky and make it taste a little better."

Sarah eyed the four of them. "How can you all joke at a time like this?"

The Kid turned and it seemed as though

someone hit him in his lean belly with the flat of a pick handle. "A joke don't hurt none, ma'am," he said.

"With all those dead men lying out there?" she demanded.

"Apaches," said Bung. He spat inelegantly to one side.

"I meant those soldiers," she said.

"Yankees," said Chet.

Theresa looked at him. "I might have known," she said. "Rebels."

Chet smiled coldly. "I wear the name," he said. "I find no dishonour in it."

"The war has been over for eight years," she said.

Chet turned to the Kid. "Harness the Yankee horses to the team," he said. "Take the leaders. They're the fastest. *Andele!*" He turned on a heel and walked to where they had left their meagre gear. He did not look back.

"What did I do wrong?" asked Theresa as she began to cleanse the ragged wound with a piece of frilled cloth from the hem of her petticoat wet with water from the tank.

Bung winced a little. "He ain't forgot," he said.

"You served with him?"

"Yes."

"And the other one? The Kid?"

Bung shook his head. "His pappy was killed alongside us at Chickamauga. He's only twenty years old, ma'am. Me and Chet we kind'a adopted him after the war. It was Chet taught him how to fight. Did you see him with those sixguns out there?" Bung's voice rang with admiration.

Sarah had seated herself beside the shallow tank. She dabbled a slim hand in the water. Her face was still white and tense. The harsh memory of that dawn would stay with her for life like an invisible scar. "Killing," she said.

"What else?" said Bung hotly. "You know what would have happened to you if we didn' come out shooting? Wasn't my idea. Weren't Chet's either for that matter. It was the Kid's! All me and Chet wanted was hosses!"

Theresa's hand dropped. She stared uncomprehendingly at the big man. "You mean saving us was only incidental?"

Bung flushed deeply. "Well," he said weakly.

"Shut up," said Chet King as he reappeared. He threw the gear on the ground and handed Theresa the bottle of Abyssinian Companion.

"Take it easy with this stuff, ma'am. Burns like fire."

She nodded. Chet felt for the makings and rolled a cigarette. His grey eyes flicked at the taller of the two women now and then. There was a cold set look on her lovely face. "How far is it to El Paso?" she asked Bung.

"'Bout thirty miles."

She bandaged his shoulder and recorked the bottle. "Are the Apaches gone?"

"Them that ain't dead." Bung looked curiously at her. "You figuring on riding into El Paso? Just the two of you?"

"I can drive," she said.

"That swiftwagon is fair bait for any 'Paches that might be watching the road, ma'am."

"We can't stay here," she said quietly.

Bung looked at Chet and shrugged. Both of them knew they'd better not stick their noses into El Paso, and that went for the Kid as well.

The sun was flooding the desert when the Kid came hurriedly into the tanks. "Dust from the east," he said.

Chet picked up his battered fieldglasses, relic of the war, and climbed up a rock slope. He focussed the glasses. The sun glinted from metal and he could make out the dusty blue of uniforms. A lot of uniforms. Full company of cavalry at least, probably from Fort Concho, or perhaps Davis. He looked to the south. Dust was spiralling up from a hard riding knot of horsemen, but they weren't soldiers. Rangers probably, either trailing Chet and his amigos, or perhaps they had heard the gunfire and were investigating. He looked to the west. More dust. This time raised by several wagons, a stagecoach and a group of civilian horsemen. Employees of the Southern Overland in all likelihood. It was no time to make positive identification.

Chet slid down the rocks and jerked his head at Bung. "Soldiers from the east; horsemen, likely Rangers from the south; more horsemen and some wagons from the west, probably Southern Overland men."

Bung tightened the cinch on his gelding. "That leaves the north," he said.

"And more Apaches," said the Kid.

"I'll chance them," said Bung. "We can kill *them* without facing a noose. Right, Chet?"

"Keno!" Chet slid his Winchester into its scabbard and swung up on his horse. He tipped his hat. "We hate to leave you two ladies to the tender mercies of Yankee cavalry, but we aren't exactly popular with them."

"Or the Texas Rangers," added the Kid with a grin.

"Or the Guardia Rurale," said Bung. He mounted.

"Lead that extra horse, Kid," said Chet. "We can have a good lead by the time the blue-bellies get here."

Theresa Case walked to Chet and held out a slim hand. "I'm sorry if I offended you," she said. "Thanks again for saving us from that." She shuddered a little. "We live in New Mexico Territory, Chet. At Two Rivers. My father is Bart Case. It doesn't mean much now, but if you ever need anything, please come to Two Rivers. My father will be glad to help you."

Chet tipped his hat. "Gracias." He touched his horse with his spurs and rode towards the entrance to the tanks. He turned in his saddle. "We could have gotten the horses *after* they were through with you, ma'am. Please remember that." Then he was gone.

The kid smiled and Theresa's heart warmed to him. The Kid rode up beside Sarah. She stood up and brushed back a stray lock of her blonde hair. She never expected him to lean from his saddle and kiss her cheek. Then he was gone too.

Bung slapped his horse on the rump. "Comin', Cap'n!" he said. He grinned widely. "Don't let them Yankee soldiers talk you into anythin', ladies." He spurred after the Kid.

Theresa walked to the entrance and watched the three of them riding north into the hostile desert. She didn't see Chet King as he was, dressed in dusty trail clothing and battered hat, but rather in faded Confederate grey, with perhaps a bullet hole raggedly patched here and there, with the three gold bars of a captain stitched on each side of the collar, and the twin galloons of gold on each lower sleeve.

She was still standing there when the three parties of horsemen arrived almost simultaneously at the stage station. Soldiers from the east; Texas Rangers from the south; Southern Overland men from the west.

She told the story to the three leaders. It was the sergeant of Texas Rangers who settled the matter. "They're on their way out of Texas," he said quietly. "We owe them a few hours start for what they did here."

"Amen," said the cavalry officer.

The Southern Overland man nodded. "I can write off the two horses they took."

The cavalry officer looked at the carnage of the little battlefield. "They fought like demons," he said.

Theresa Case looked quickly at him. "Not demons, Captain McCann. Rather like Confederate veterans."

"I see," he said drily. Then he smiled. "Thank God *we* aren't still fighting *them*."

The thin thread of dust was rising higher and higher against the clear blue of the morning sky and the sun was already beginning to beat down on the naked desert.

The steadily riding trio crossed the New Mexico line by midmorning though there was no sign of it. The country was all the same, harsh and naked, brooding and beaten by the merciless sun. Far ahead of them the hazy outline of the Sacramentos arose like the recumbent bulk of some huge prehistoric monster.

They rode slowly but steadily all that day, riding an hour, walking an hour, conserving their water, and tightening their belts for a Spanish lunch. They reached a water hole at the edge of the barren mountains at dusk. They silently ate the last of the beans and bacon, and

29

drank the last weak potful of Arbuckles, before they rolled their smokes, and sat with their backs against the warm rocks, all occupied with their own thoughts.

"How far is Colorado?" asked Bung at last.

"Two hundred and fifty miles maybe," said Chet.

"Arizona?" asked the Kid.

"Probably less than two hundred," said Chet. He sucked in on his cigarette and they could see his lean hawk's face lighted by the glowing of the tip.

"Texis is due west," said Bung. "Damned Panhandle goes plumb up to the Nations." He rolled another cigarette. "Which way, Chet?"

"*Más alla*. Farther on."

"Which way, Chet?" said the Kid.

Chet dipped two fingers into his pocket and plucked out a pair of 'dobe dollars and a silver eagle. "This is all I got," he said. "How do you two stand?"

Bung spread out his huge hands, palms upwards. "*Nada*," he said.

"Kid?"

The Kid flipped a coin into the air. "One centavo with a clipped edge and teeth marks on it."

"No chow, no dinero, not a damned thing but saddle sore and a helluva appetite," said Bung gloomily.

"We've got to go to work," said Chet at last.

"Perish forbid," said Bung.

The Kid dug between his teeth with a wood splinter. "Any chance of cashing in our Colts?"

Chet shrugged. "We can't go back to Mexico, or Texas either. If we get on the wrong side of the law here in New Mexico our luck will surely run out."

"So?"

Chet tilted his head to one side. "Why not stay on the right side of the law?"

"He's been out in the sun too long," said Bung.

The Kid narrowed his eyes. "No," he said. "Say on, Chet."

"All day long I've been trying to associate the name Case with something I remembered from years ago. Bart Case. It came to me a little while ago."

"Go on," said Bung.

Chet looked up at them. "Bart Case is a big man in New Mexico. Ranch owner. Businessman. Ex-Territorial Representative.

War veteran. Happens also to be the local sheriff in his bailiwick."

"I'm beginning to see the light," said the Kid.

"Tell me," said Bung. "I'm out in the dark and cold."

"We saved his daughter and his niece, didn't we?" said Chet. "The old man ought'a be obliged."

"For a handout like?" said Bung.

"For more than a handout," said Chet. "Old Man Case runs his part of the territory with a mailed fist from what I hear tell. Maybe he can use a trio of gunfighters."

"Sounds fair," said the Kid.

"I don't like the idea of working for anyone," said Bung. "I'm my own man."

"Yeh," jeered the Kid. "Look at you! Holes in your socks and holes in your boots. You can read a newspaper through the seat of your jeans if you hold them up against the light."

"I still like to work by my own," stubbornly insisted Bung.

Chet shrugged. "All right. Is it Arizona or Colorado?"

"Colorado," said Bung.

"Kid?"

The Kid hesitated. "I'm partial to Arizona but I ain't against hitting Old Man Case for beans and bacon, and a job."

"What about you, Chet?" said Bung quietly.

"I already gave you my idea."

The big man heaved himself to his feet and rubbed his bandaged shoulder softly. "Two against one," he said.

"I'll toss for it," said the Kid.

Chet stood up. The moon was just peering over the distant Guadalupes. He quickly took the silver eagle and poised it on a thumbnail, cocking the nail under the first finger. "Heads we go to Colorado; tails to Two Rivers. Keno?"

"Keno," said the Kid.

Bung nodded.

Chet flipped the coin. It spun upward, catching the light of the moon on its polished surfaces. Chet caught it deftly and slapped it hard on his left wrist. He glanced at it. "Tails," he said.

"Best out of three?" said Bung.

"You should have said that before I tossed, Bungo," said Chet easily. He pocketed the coin and drew out the makings. He rolled a cigarette impassively while Bung eyed him suspiciously. The big man was suspicious but he'd never challenge Chet or name him cheat. Chet walked out of the rock enclosure to check the horses. It wasn't the first time he had cheated the big man, and the Kid too for that matter, for their own good.

He stood out in the clear moonlight looking north, puffing slowly at his cigarette. Her eyes were hazel, or maybe more brown flecked with gold. Her hair was dark and glossy almost with a tint of blue to it. Her mouth wide and soft. He remembered other things too. Things he had seen and could not forget as she struggled nakedly on the hard ground. He forced them from his mind.

The night wind began to rise, swirling away the sluggish heat of the day. Chet walked back to the waterhole. Both his companions were wrapped in their blankets. He picked up his rifle and scaled the steep slope behind the camp. From where he was he could see the silvery desert and the distant mountains. He cut a chew and settled himself. A coyote lifted its cry from somewhere out in the desert. Its utter loneliness came to Chet King, and the man was no less lonely than the animal.

3

FAR to the west were dead mesas of purple lava lying stark against the saffron and grey of the desert. To the north were low green clouds of cottonwoods against bronze red hills that rose at the foot of smokey blue mountains fanged with sharp edged peaks. Everything was vague and unreal to the eye because of the constantly shifting haze that covered the land. The heat and dryness of the wind drove moisture from everything except the tough greasewood and the grey-green sage brush.

The three horsemen topped a naked ridge and all of them drew rein as though at a silent command. The sudden transition from the heat and dryness of the desert land stretching far behind them was almost too much for men whose water had run out the evening before. They had given the horses the last of it and had ridden and walked all day across the *jornado* with pebbles in their dry mouths in a vain attempt to start a quenching flow of saliva.

The sun glinted brightly from *acequias* that

35

flowed through the green fields from the *madre acequia* or mother irrigation ditch. Cottonwoods and willows waved gracefully in the dry wind reflecting themselves in the running water. The fields were green with vegetables and fruits. Oleanders raised their flower tipped greenery not far from apricot trees with their sprays of leaves.

There were many houses following the winding road that passed through the wide valley to vanish into the narrow mouth of a pass through which flowed a shallow river that parralleled the dusty road and fed the *madre acequia*. There was another river far across the green fields, winding in and out of bosques of cottonwoods. The two rivers met at the very southern end of the valley and flowed further south.

A flock of pigeons rose from a cote and flowed across the fields like a living cloud. A scarf of bluish smoke hovered over the houses and as the wind shifted a little it carried the enticing odour of food to the three tired, thirsty men sitting their horses on the ridge.

"I don't believe it," said Bung in a thirst cracked voice.

"Must have got lost somewhere," said the Kid. He blinked his sun reddened eyes.

Chet King took the cigarette from his lips, wincing as the paper tore the cracked skin. "No," he said quietly. "I was here right after the war. Place didn't look like this then. Because of the fighting between the Yankees and the Texicans for possession of the Territory, the Apaches raised hell all around here. The New Mexicans could hardly hold them off. There was a time when this valley was practically deserted. Looks like they've been busy rebuilding since the war."

"Done a good job too," said Bung. He sniffed the dry air mingled with the odour of rich food. "By God! I could do with a horse bucket full of chile and beans."

Chet rode down towards the dusty road. It was Two Rivers all right. He had forgotten being there so many years ago. Two Rivers! He'd see Theresa Case again. Chet and his amigos had made a slow passage from the south because of Apache scares in the mountain valleys. They had sold one of the horses for oats, beans, and bacon.

The late afternoon sun was slanting down into the valley shining on the soft warm colours of the adobe houses, various shades of pink, brown, salmon, and yellow. It sparkled from the crosses of bright stones that had been formed against the wet adobe walls of the houses when they had been built. Scarlet *ristras* of chiles, red as rubies, hung in great strings against the sides of the houses mingled with great bundles of onions like balls of mother of pearl. Corn, hay, and golden pumpkins lay on the flat roofs drying in the hot sun.

As the three dusty men rode towards the edge of the little town the clear high bugle notes of the prairie lark rose from near a large earthen water tank. The chuckling of the running water in the ditch that flowed alongside the road was too much for the horses. The three men sat in their saddles as the horses drank. Chet rolled a quirly and passed the makings on to the others. None of the men drank, dry as they were. It was Bung who voiced their restraint. "I ain't drinking anything but a tall cold beer, if they got such a thing in this *placita*," he said. He wiped dust from his mouth with the hairy back of his hand.

"Amen," said the Kid.

"Think we ought to let him have a beer, Chet?" asked Bung.

Chet spat drily. "Last time he got likkered up we had to finish his fight for him."

The Kid flushed beneath the mask of dusk. "Well it was poisoned likker or something," he said angrily.

"Sure was," said Bung drily. "Poisoned that simple brain of yours. It was twenty-four hours later when you come to out in the *mala tierra* with a head twice too big for you, and no knowledge of the mess we had to clean up for you."

"We'll let him have a spoonful at stated intervals," said Chet. He kneed his horse away from the water.

The scent of autumn was in the New Mexican air. Thyme and sage, mint and ripened corn mingled with the rich odour of cooking food drifting along the quiet road.

Within a hundred yards of the rounded *torreon*, the thick walled tower, loop holed and barred with a thick door studded with nails, for defence against Apaches, the trio underwent a change. They straightened in their saddles, slapped some of the dust from their clothing with their hats, eased their holstered sixguns further forward, pulled their hats level with their eyes, and kept their cigarettes in the

39

corners of their mouths. They were Anglos entering a town of the past; a town that had been old when Chicago was a trading post and Americans were casting thoughtful looks west of the Mississippi. They were Anglos, and they were *Texans*, and the nickname *Texican* was spat out like an oath by the men of New Mexico. They had reason to do so. The war was not that long in the past. In '62 the men of Sibley's Brigade had penetrated as far north as Santa Fe and had captured it after defeating the Yankees at Valverde to the south. A drawn battle in Glorieta Pass had stopped them, but the men who had stopped them had been mostly Regulars and Coloradoans, not native New Mexicans. Only the destruction of their supply train and horse herd had forced the Texicans back to the south in a bitter retreat. It had ended the use of Texas as a springboard for the invasion of the Pacific Coast. It had been the greatest single Texas exploit of the war. It might have succeeded. Certainly it had not failed because of lack of Texas blood and guts. Yes, the Texans were well remembered in New Mexico. Too well . . .

So a Texan riding through New Mexico, more than ten years after the invasion, did well to keep alert. One Texan had to have eyes in the back of his head; two Texans could stand back to back; three Texans, in their opinion of course, could have easily handled another invasion. For men who'd charge hell with a bucket of water, it should be a simple matter. So the three Texans slid into their go-to-hell looks an instant before the first of the townspeople knew them for what they were.

Several bare-butted toddlers fled for cover. Older women covered their faces with their shawls and silently vanished. The younger women indolently moved away, but quite a few of them flashed quick smiles over a bare brown shoulder. It was the men who gave the *placita* its air of foreboding silence. Men whose ordinarily liquid brown eyes seemed to have congealed into hard amber. Brown fingers felt for hidden knives, but only when the level-eyed Texans were looking elsewhere. Those gringos could shoot faster than *uiboras cascabeles*, the rattlesnake could strike.

"What?" said Bung in simulated horror. "No brass band? No rifle salutes? No flags?"

The others did not answer. The Kid was too busy looking at the dusty brown legs of the girls or at the swellings beneath their thin cotton blouses. Here and there along the street the brightly painted doors were shut, or the shutters of the small and secretive windows were closed. Pigs grunted away from the forelegs of the three horses. Dogs slunk for cover, turning now and then to bare yellowed teeth in a mirthless grin.

They entered the plaza, dusty and still bright with sunlight. A dry fountain stood in the middle beside a rickety paint peeling band stand. A monte dealer looked up from his blanket spread on the hard ground, then looked quickly away. He wanted no part of these men. One crooked deal and he'd end up with his guts spilling into his bloody hands after a bowie had sliced across his belly, or die kicking like a beheaded chicken with a softnosed slug in his chest.

There was a change at the north end of the plaza. Instead of the earthen buildings of the Mexican Colonial Period, with their bright colours of pink and blue, orchid yellow and yeso-white, there was a long row of false fronted wooden buildings, with the painted walls faded and the unpainted walls silvered and warped by the hot suns. A ramada hung over the earthen sidewalk and beneath it the town idlers sat on benches backed against the dusty display windows of the stores. A pair of batwings swung back and forth as a thirsty cowpoke pushed his way into a saloon.

"That's for me," said Bung.

They crossed the plaza and tethered their tired horses to the hitching rail, then walked with jingling spurs and popping boot heels into the dark interior of the saloon to rest tired elbows on the high mahogany bar and to hook a bootheel on the brass footrail.

"Tres cervezas, amigo!" said Bung.

"Don't talk spic in here, friend," said the baldheaded barcritter.

Bung shrugged. "I thought we was in New Mexico."

The bartender drew three. "You are. Maybe you forgot New Mexico became part of the United States about twenty-five years ago."

"Well, I'll be dipped!" said Bung in astonishment. "You don't say!"

"I do say." The bartender placed the glasses in front of the three Texans. He eyed them. "Texas men?"

"Yep," said the Kid. "Any objections?"

"None," said the barkeep hastily. "I'm an Arkansas man myself."

"Never heard of it," said the Kid calmly as he raised his glass.

The few men in the place looked up and eyed the three strangers, then as quickly looked away again. They had no belly for looking eye to eye with such men.

Chet finished his second beer. "Where can I find Bart Case?" he asked.

"He might be in his office," said the bartender. "Major Case usually works until after dark."

"*Major* Case?" said Chet.

"Well you can call him sheriff, or mister, or anything you like, but most of us call him major."

"From the War?"

The bartender nodded. "First New Mexico Volunteers."

"Yankees?" said Bung loudly.

Chet pressed a boot toe hard on the big man's foot.

Several of the other customers looked up again, this time with harder looks in their eyes.

The bartender refilled their glasses. "Kit Carson's regiment," he said casually. "They fought like tigers at Valverde Fords in '62."

"Tigers," said the Kid. "Maybe paper tigers like the Chinks have?"

The bartender was a peaceable man, and a diplomat, like most of his trade, but he was also a man of courage. "Seems like the Confederates from Texas left a little faster than they come," he said quietly.

"Amen," said Chet. "Where's Major Case's office?"

"To your right as you leave. Sheriff's office. You can't miss it. Barred windows."

"To keep him in, or others out?" said Bung.

The bartender shrugged. "Major Case is a big man around here, mister. A *big* man . . ." He walked to the other end of the bar to serve a customer.

Chet looked at his two grinning companions. "Listen, and listen well," he said coldly. "I'm going to see the major right now. I'll be back in an hour. By God, if you two get likkered up and start a fight, I'll leave you here to get licked."

"Hear him!" jeered the Kid.

"You heard me," said Chet. He drained his beer and left the bar. The sun was gone as he walked along beneath the long ramada. Only the tips of the distant peaks were still lighted by

45

the dying sun. Smoke from cooking fires drifted across the plaza, with a pleasing astringent odour to it. A burro brayed. A dog barked. Somewhere off the plaza the soft tone of a church bell rang out and echoed from the nearby hills.

Men watched the tall gringo as he walked along the side of the plaza. They watched him enter the sheriff's office, and some of them nodded their heads. It was not the first time such a man had come from the desert, dusty and trail worn, to see Major Case. Cold-eyed men with well-worn gun butts and death in their hard eyes. Such men kept Bart Case in power.

Chet opened an inner door and looked into a semi-dark room dominated by a huge roll top desk. The odour of cigar smoke was thick in the place. A man sat by the barred window, looking out across the shadowy plaza, with a slim cigar held between his teeth. He did not move, though he surely must have heard Chet enter.

"Major Case?" asked Chet.

The man nodded.

"The name is Chet King."

The cigar worked from one side of the mouth

to the other. "And the other two are Bung and the Kid, eh?"

Chet narrowed his eyes. How could he have found out?

"I know more than my daughter does then," said Case drily. "All she called you was Chet. Chet King, eh?"

"She's here then?"

The man nodded. "Both of them. By God, I should have never let them go to Texas."

"Anything wrong with Texas?" challenged Chet.

The head shook. "Not for me, King. If you like it so much, what are you doing in New Mexico, looking for a job?"

Chet grinned. "You hit a soft spot there, Major Case."

"Bung?" said the major musingly. "What the hell kind of handle is that for a big man to wear?"

"Short for Bungstarter," said Chet. "A nickname."

"I imagine," said the major. "Why Bungstarter?"

"If you ever saw him hit a man, sir, you'd know he seems to carry a bungstarter in each fist."

47

"And the other one? The Kid?"

"He travels with us."

"Theresa said he handles sixguns like a fighting machine."

"He does."

"You taught him?"

Chet hesitated.

"You don't have to answer that, King. I know your breed. You three want jobs?"

"That's the general idea, sir."

Case turned his head a little, enough for Chet to see a thick moustache and a beak of a nose in profile against the lighter area of the window. "What do you want to do?"

Chet shrugged. "Damned near anything."

"I have range land, a few mine properties, farm land, businesses here in town, and in other *placitas*. You a vaquero? Miner? Farmer? Businessman?" snapped out the major.

Chet leaned against the side of the door. "You in need of vaqueros? Miners? Farmers? Businessmen?" He laughed. "I get the impression you need *fighting* men, Major Case."

"Who told you that?"

"I've heard of you. You run this part of New Mexico like the old time *patrons* used to run it.

48

Not without some difficulty from certain parties however. Men like you make enemies, Major Case, no matter how many titles you have. Discounting your war record, your service in the Territorial Legislature and that as sheriff, you still have enemies. You can't fight 'em all alone, major."

"You're a little blunt and to the point, Mister King."

Chet laughed again. "I have the impression that you talk the same way, sir."

Case turned. His face was still in shadow but when he drew in on the cigar the glowing tip lighted the square face, the thick grey-white dragoon style moustache, the beak of a nose. "I'll take you on, King, and your two friends. Theresa's story was enough for me. Thanks to you three men I have my daughter and my beloved niece back with me. You're hired, starting on the payroll as of today. Fifty a month and found for the other two, a hundred a month and expenses for you."

"Why the difference?" asked Chet quietly.

"They'll be on the payroll of Case Enterprises. I have another spot for you." Case stood up and felt in a drawer. "Raise your right hand, King." In two minutes Chet King, Texan, unreconstructed rebel, outlaw, and fugitive, had been sworn in as deputy sheriff of that county, Territory of New Mexico. He felt the weight of the star as Case pinned it to his shirt and then stepped back. "Easy, wasn't it?" said the major.

Chet looked down at the star. "A little illegal, isn't it?" he said.

"Any objections?"

"None."

Case waved a hand. "Then don't worry about it."

"You take long chances, major."

Case relighted his cigar and in the quick spurt of light from the match Chet saw steady grey eyes holding his. He also saw a thick scar alongside the left temple, that started from above the left ear. Chet had seen such scars inflicted during the war and in Mexico. Nothing but a sabre slash looked like that. Maybe the major had been a real soldier after all.

Case walked to the wall and felt for his hat. He placed it on his thick grey hair. "What regiment?" he asked.

"Eleventh Texas Calvary, Second Brigade, Wharton's Division, Cavalry Corps, Army of Tennessee."

Case nodded. "And later?"

Chet shrugged. "Mexico with Jo Shelby's unreconstructed cavalry."

"On the run since then?"

"In a manner of speaking."

"In a manner of speaking," said Case drily. "That puts it very well." He walked towards Chet, bumped the desk a little and stood near the window, puffing on his cigar. "Now, Mister King," he continued, "I don't give a fiddler's damn where you've been or who you have fought with. As of now you are a deputy sheriff in this county, subject to my orders. I have Yankees, foreigners, native New Mexicans, and a few ex-rebels on my various payrolls. I ask nothing from them but loyalty and fighting ability when I need it. I need hardly remind you that courage and fighting ability were hardly the sole characteristics of the Confederates in general and the Texans in particular, no matter how much it stings your ego, Mister King. The war has been over for eight years. We are one people now. Keep your old hatreds and differences to yourself as long as you work for me."

"And in return?" asked Chet drily.

Case turned. "I never forget men who serve me," he said. "*Never . . .*"

Chet held the door open for the major. They

walked out into the street. A lean man lounged against the front of the building. "Stoughton," said the major, "this is Chet King, a new deputy sheriff. King, this is Mark Stoughton, jailkeeper. A good man."

Chet gripped Stoughton's hand. The jail-keeper grinned. "Fast promotion, King," he said.

Chet nodded. He walked beside the major towards the long row of wooden buildings.

Case raised a hand. "Seems odd I suppose, to see wooden buildings forming one side of a *placita* square. So happens most of the buildings on this side had been burned out by the Apaches during the war. I razed them when I returned and had these structures built."

"Case Enterprises?" said Chet.

The major nodded. "They may not look like part of the sleepy old *placita*, but they are practical, and they pay me *rent*, King."

It was dark in the plaza, hardly lighted by the yellow glow of the lamps from the windows, and the older adobe buildings were tightly shuttered. Chet raised his head as they approached a side street. He glanced to right and left. Something was warning him. His sixth sense, honed by years of war and impending danger, had never failed him yet, but there was nothing to see.

Hoofs suddenly tattooed on the hard packed earth of the side street and a horseman lashed his mount towards the two men. Major Case stepped into the street directly in front of the horseman. Chet King moved like a cat. He slammed a shoulder against the older man, driving him back against the nearest building. He caught the dull glinting of steel in the horseman's right hand. He went flat and drew Colt as the pistol exploded. The slug smashed into the adobe wall directly in line with where Chet's head had been before he had gone to earth.

The major cursed and clawed beneath his black frock coat. Chet fired from the ground as the horse slammed past into the square. Once again the horseman's pistol flamed and the slug whined eerily from the hardpacked earth, inches from Chet's head. Chet's second shot raised a puff of dust from the man's coat. He swayed in the saddle, then wrenched the horse to one side and raced for the darkness of a side street.

Chet stood up and holstered his smoking Colt. He turned to see the major standing against the wall with a short-barrelled Colt in his hand. "That was close, Major Case," he said. "Too damned close to suit me."

"He was after me, King, not you."

Men were shouting in the darkness. Doors opened flooding part of the square with yellow light. Dust and powder-smoke writhed in the sudden illumination.

"This way," said the major. He led the way down the dark street and cut up the next narrow way until they reached the next street. He turned to look at Chet King. "It didn't take you long to earn your keep," he said quietly. "I'm going home now, King." He felt in his pocket and handed Chet a thick wad of bills. "You may need this for quarters and food."

"But you don't know how much it is."

"*You* will," said Case. "It's up to *you* to keep the account. If you like, you can come out to the estate for quarters. Ask for Jose Silva my ranch manager. He'll take care of you. Good night, King." The major walked off into the darkness.

Chet shrugged. He fingered the money. It had been a close thing. If Chet hadn't sensed the approach of that rider of death, Bart Case would have been lying dead in the street. Chet counted the money and his eyes widened quite a bit.

He found his two amigos standing at the bar in the saloon, all unconcerned about the excitement in the street. Even the bartender had run out into the square. "We've got jobs," said Chet. He picked up the Kid's beer glass and drained it.

Bung eyed the star on Chet's shirt. "Sold your birthright for a mess of pottage, like it says in the Good Book?"

Chet placed the bills on the damp bar. "There's the pottage," he said. "Split it three ways, Bung, or between me and the Kid if you're so finicky."

Bung grinned. "I don't know how you did it," he said, "but it's all right with me. I'm an eating man myself."

The Kid eyed Chet. "You know anything about that shooting out there?"

"Nope."

The Kid wrinkled his nose. "I smell gunsmoke," he said.

"You was born smelling gunsmoke," said Bung.

"We can eat here in town and get quarters,"

said Chet. "The Major says we can bunk out at the *estate* if we like."

The Kid rubbed his jaw. "Could do with a bath and clean bed," he said. "I'm for going out there."

"Me too," said Chet.

Bung shrugged. "With only two fillies out there, for you two studs, that leaves Ol' Bungo out in the cold."

"You can stay in town if you like," said Chet.

Bung shook his head. "Well, if they got two fillies out there, they likely got more. I always did like them little Mex gals. They ain't so fussy and they like *big* men."

The bartender came in and refilled the glasses. He glanced at the star on Chet's shirt, but there was no expression on his face. "I see you got the job," he said.

"Deputy sheriff," said the Kid. "Let's have a little respect for the law here, mister!"

The bartender smiled. "Always do. There's quite a few of them stars around this part of the country."

"How many?" said Chet.

The bartender shrugged. "Counting you, I think there's an even half dozen now."

"What does the county think about a payroll like that?"

"They don't pay for the extra ones, mister. The major does, and don't you ever forget it."

"Like a private army, eh?" said the Kid a little loosely. He hiccupped.

"Sort of," admitted the man. He watched them when they left, with his slatey eyes. "Texicans!" he said when the batwings swung behind them. "That's all we need around here!"

4

THE new moon was shining down on the valley of the Two Rivers, glinting from the water in the pools and irrigation ditches. There was a warm softness in the night air. The hoofs of the three horses struck the hard road in a steady tattoo that echoed from the nearby hills. In the distance, with its base buried in shrubbery and screened by a tracery of gently waving trees was the big white *casa* of Bart Case. A windmill whirred steadily in the wind.

Now and then Chet King turned in his saddle, resting a hand on the cantle, to look back along the white track of the road, lighted by the moon. The road was deserted except for the three Texans and the shifting shadows of the tall trees that bordered the road between it and the irrigation ditches on either hand, but to Chet King there was a brooding quality about that road and the country through which they were passing. Yet it had always seemed so to Chet, on many roads, in many places, from

58

Tennessee to Mexico. Always as though he was being watched, and in being watched he must be extra watchful. Danger always seemed to ride close herd on Chet King.

Who was the man he had wounded that evening in the plaza? The man had meant to kill Bart Case, there was no doubt about that in Chet's mind. He looked down at the bright metal star pinned to his last clean shirt, bumping gently against his chest. He had accepted this sudden office because he felt as though he was joining in some fantastic game of profit and loss as well as danger. A man can't reach the age of thirty without wondering where his future lies, and cursing the wasted past. Somehow he knew this might be the last wild cast of the dice before he vanished into the shadows of later life. A cast of the dice that might make all the difference between failure and success, with sudden and violent death as the possible penalty for failure.

He glanced at his two companions. Their bellies were full. They had just enough liquor in them to make them forget their troubles. They had money in their jeans and jobs that might make them a handsome profit if the cards fell the right way. That was the rub. If the cards failed them, they'd likely die along with Chet.

Theresa Case might have the answers. At least she might have reassurance for him, for he knew well enough it was Theresa who had made the small miracle possible in having him deputized the first hour he was in Two Rivers. Sometimes he was apt to forget the implications in the memory of her eyes; eyes flecked with dancing gold. Perhaps it was the gold in her lovely eyes he really wanted rather than the cold metal itself. There are values and there are values, and a man must make his choice and live with it for the rest of his life.

They saw the entrance to the Case rancho ahead of them on the road, beyond a bridge that spanned the river. A man stepped out from the shadows to watch them. A rifle was held in the crook of his arm. He waited for them as they rattled across the bridge and as he looked up at Chet he moved the rifle to cover him. "Who are you?" he said. "What do you want?"

"Chet King. These are my *companeros*. Major Case said we could come out to the ranch for quarters. I was to ask for Jose Silva."

The guard lowered his rifle. "Adolfo," he said, "Keep watch while I go with these men."

60

"We can find the way, amigo," said Bung.

The man turned. "There are others on guard," he said.

"Like getting into a dingdanged fortress," said the Kid.

The dark face of the guard was fully revealed by the moonlight as he turned. "Yes, it is. The *patron* doesn't like strangers around here." He walked to a horse and mounted it, leading the three Texans along a shadowed road towards the distant house gleaming in the silvery light.

It was a pleasant place thought Chet. A place fit for a king. He looked about as he rode. It was almost as though he had found the place of his dreams. He smiled a little as he rolled a cigarette. An unreconstructed rebel, thirty years of age, with nothing but wound scars and the ability to kill like a professional were all he had to show for his life. The few dollars he had in his jeans were the pay of a mercenary; a hired gun.

Several men lounged around the entrance to a long, low bunkhouse set amongst the trees. "Where is Senor Jose?" asked the guide.

"I am here, Santiago," called out a tall, broad-shouldered man who stood near the beginning of the gravelled pathway that led to the side of the big house.

"These men wish to see you."

Jose walked towards them. The moonlight shone on the gilt buttons of his short jacket. His face was shielded by the wide, upturned brim of the steeple hat he wore.

"Jesusita," said the Kid in a low voice. "Adolfo, Jose and Santiago! I thought we were in the United States."

"This is New Mexico," said Bung. "Remember?"

"Another thing, Kid," said Chet. "These men are *Americans*. No matter their name, or language, or ways of doing things. They are Americans. Keep that in your craw."

"Maybe it's morn' we are," said Bung. "I ain't taken no oath of allegiance yet."

"You might have to," said Chet.

Bung looked quickly at Chet and his broad face darkened with a swift rush of blood. "By God," he said in a low voice. "I never thought to hear *you* say that!" He studied Chet's hatchet face and what he saw on it was enough to make him wonder whether or not he should have pushed on to Colorado alone, and to hell with old war comrades!

Silva looked up at them. "Good evening," he said. "Senors King, Bung, and the Kid." He laughed softly. "I like those names."

The Kid spat to one side. "They ain't funny," he said.

Chet kicked the Kid's leg. "Major Case said we could have quarters out here if we liked. The quarters in town were all occupied."

"So?" The man smiled. "That is strange. There is usually a room or two to be had. Occupied, you say?"

"Mice, cockroaches, and fleas," said the Kid.

Silva nodded. "That is true." He looked over his shoulder. "There is a small building there that is no longer used. There are cots in it, a fireplace. I will send in bedding. Is there anything else you wish?"

It was all so easy. Too easy to settle Chet's peace of mind. He looked beyond Silva. A woman had come out onto the terrace at one side of the house and stood there looking towards the distant moonlighted mountains, soft looking and peaceful.

Chet swung down from his horse and handed the reins to the Kid. "Take care of things," he said. He started for the house.

"Where are you going?" asked Silva sharply.

Chet turned with a faint smile on his face. "To see Miss Theresa," he said.

"You will have to be announced."

Chet smiled again, a little more faintly. "I can take care of that," he said softly.

Silva hesitated. "It is not proper," he said.

"Hear him," said the Kid. "Go on, Chet."

Silva held up a hand. "It is not my ruling," he said. "The *patron* is very strict about such matters." He approached Chet and walked with him towards the house. He looked sideways at the tall Texan. "It is said a man was found dead on the road the other side of the *placita*. A man with a bullet hole in his back."

Chet shrugged. "Too bad." He glanced sideways. "Shot himself by accident maybe?"

Silva laughed softly. "In the back, amigo? In the *back?*"

They reached the terrace wall. "Senorita Theresa?" said Silva.

She turned and Chet's heart seemed to skip a beat. She was dressed in white, her thick dark hair done up in Indian chongo style, a rather daring headdress for the times. It suited her well. Maybe it suited the Indian blood in Chet King himself. He took off his battered hat and

64

bowed a little. "Chet King," he said. "I trust I did not startle you, ma'am."

She came to the wall and smiled. "It's all right, Jose. Mister King is an old acquaintance of mine." She held out a hand to Chet.

Silva walked away, and neither one of them saw the hard, dark glance he shot back over his shoulder.

She looked at the star on his chest. "My father told me he had deputized you, Chet."

"Fast work," he said. "I have you to thank for that." He stepped over the wall and stood facing her and the warmth and sweetness of her presence almost hit him like a pick handle. He felt like an oaf from out in the tornillo brush as he stood there rather than Chester Fitzgerald King, Southern gentleman, ex-captain, Eleventh Texas Cavalry, CSA.

She studied him. "Did it surprise you?"

"Yes."

"I told you, back there at Hueco Tanks, that my father's name didn't mean much to you then, but that if you ever needed anything you must come here to Two Rivers. It was not to raise false hopes within you, Chet."

He looked down at the star. "It happened so quickly I am still confused."

"The man who tried to kill my father would have done so if you hadn't been there to save his life."

"I would have done it anyway, Miss Theresa."

She tilted her lovely head to one side. "Really?" she said softly. "A *Yankee?*"

He laughed. "You might have a point," he said.

She walked to the end of the terrace and placed her hands on the adobe wall, looking again at the distant mountains. "My father needs good men beside him," she said over her shoulder.

"He seems to have plenty of them," he said.

"None to take his place."

He stared at her. She had caught him completely off guard. "What do you mean by that?" he quietly asked.

She turned and faced him, placing her hands on the wall at each side of her and the effect was to make her young breasts stand out and he remembered all too well when he had seen them free of any covering back there at Hueco Tanks in the cold light of the dawn. If he had wondered at all why he had come to Two Rivers, he was quite sure at this moment.

"My father has many men," she said in a low voice. "Good fighting men. Men who give their complete loyalty to him."

"Nice, if you can do it," he said drily.

"Didn't you have such loyalty from the men who served under you in the war?"

He grinned. "Not *all* of them. You can't please them all, and a commanding officer must be as hard as a diamond to do his job right."

She nodded. "I know that. But these New Mexicans, the ones of Mexican descent at any rate, treat my father like a feudal lord. It's easy enough if you pay for the funerals."

He looked at her curiously. "I don't follow you."

"To a native New Mexican, paying for the funeral of his father or mother, wife, sister or brother, so that they may rest in peace, is enough to have his friendship and loyalty for life."

"And the Anglos who work for the major?"

She smiled. "You wear the star," she said. "You have his money in your pocket, with the knowledge that there is much more of it to come. It's as simple as that."

"Doesn't anyone serve the man for himself?"

She looked quickly at him. Her lips parted.

She looked away. "I do," she said in a low voice.

There was no restraint in him, moonlight or no moonlight, boss's daughter or not. He drew her close and found her soft full lips, crushing them hungrily. She did not resist. Her arms crept about his neck and she returned his passion kiss for kiss, until at last she broke free, breathing hard, her face flushed. She touched her hair here and there and looked quickly about. "You shouldn't have done that, Chet," she murmured.

"You didn't struggle very hard, Theresa."

She walked into the shadows beneath the ramada roof. She turned. "I think you know now why I wanted you to come here, Chet. My father needs a righthand man upon whom he can trust his life. If that man measures up to my father's standards, there is no limit upon how far he can go. Remember that, Chet." She kissed him quickly and vanished into the big house.

Chet walked to the wall and stepped over it. The taste of her kisses were still sweet as honey on his desert cracked lips and the aura of her hair and body seemed to cling to him, to haunt him with deep longing as he walked, almost blindly to his quarters.

Bung was sprawled on his bunk and the Kid was building a fire in the corner beehive fireplace against the coming chill of the later night. They looked curiously at him. "You see the old man?" asked Bung.

"No."

"Maybe you better."

"Why?"

Bung reached under the far side of the bunk and came up with a squat dark bottle. He drank deeply. "Chihuahua!" he gasped. "Seems like the town marshal come in to see the major. Something about a killing in Two Rivers this evening."

Chet leaned against the wall, still occupied with his thoughts of Theresa, while he rolled a cigarette. "So?"

Bung's eyes flicked at the Kid, then at Chet. "Seems like the man who was killed was quite the boyo around the valley."

"Get to the point!" snapped Chet.

The Kid looked curiously at Chet. He hunkered on his heels and began to fashion a smoke.

Bung wiped his mouth and sat up. "Seems like he has a family. Three brothers and a coupla cousins who are, as the saying goes, demanding justice."

"They name names?"

Bung grinned. "Half a dozen men say it was you who done the job."

"He was trying to kill the major."

"Who says so?" asked the Kid.

Chet's face darkened. His glance was like the blow of a quirt. "*I* say so!"

Bung shrugged. He looked at the star. "I wonder if any of these accusers know you was deputized a coupla minutes before you killed that hombre?"

"Like a personal bodyguard to the major," said the Kid. He laughed as he lighted his cigarette with a splinter from the fire.

"Jose told us the relatives of the dead man are hard case, Chet. Real gunslingers. Hard as nails. And they ain't exactly friends with the major, or any of his *hired* help," said Bung.

"So?" said Chet.

"We got horses, full bellies, enough dinero to make it to Colorado, if we leave now."

"Or Arizona," echoed the Kid.

Chet King's mind was more concerned with Theresa Case than with the men who were looking for him to pay a blood debt.

"Well?" said Bung.

"I'm staying," said Chet.

"Kid," said Bung.

"Ain't hardly had time to get used to this place yet," said the Kid. "Besides, you and me ain't earned the cash we got from the old man."

"Only a damned fool would stay here now," said Bung.

The kid yawned. He again looked curiously at Chet. "Oh, I don't know."

Chet flipped his cigarette into the fireplace. "Where are they now?" he asked.

"Up at the big casa," said Bung. "Whilst you was fooling around in the moonlight with the darkhaired filly, they come up to the gate. The old man sent word they could come up to the house. He said he wanted you there too."

Chet walked to the doorway.

"Wait," said the Kid. "I'll go along."

"No," said Chet sharply. He left the room.

The Kid glanced at Bung. "What's the matter with him?"

Bung took another drink. "I ain't sure. Maybe it's that filly. She'd bother anyone, Kid."

The Kid grinned. "Looks like there might yet be some excitement around here, Bungo."

"Without a doubt," said Bung drily.

"You still want to pull out?"

Bung lay back on the bunk and stared at the ceiling. "I ain't sure. I got a foreboding, Kid. We three been together quite a spell. Just damned fool luck we ain't been broken up."

"You mean by bullets?"

Bung turned his head. "Yeh," he said softly. "By bullets. That's exactly what I meant."

The Kid looked down into the crackling fire. He didn't believe a word Bung had said.

5

CHET could hear the low, hard voices in the living room of the house as he was shown to the door of the room by the lithe Mexican girl, hardly more than sixteen or seventeen, whose liquid brown eyes held an unspoken invitation to the big Texan. Chet paused in the doorway, removing his hat. Four men faced Major Case. The ranch owner stood with his back to the low fire in the massive fireplace, calmly facing the quartet in front of him.

"By God, Case!" said the tallest of the four men. "This is too much! Benny was shot down in cold blood by this unknown Texican you claim works for you! By God! Did you hire him *before* or *after* he killed my brother!"

"You call me *Major* Case, Tibbetts," said the major.

"I got a good mind to find that killer and haul him into town by his heels!"

"Let's go get 'im, Charley," eagerly said the shortest of the men.

"I let you men onto my place in peace," said the major. "I expect you to depart that way as well."

"Now, major," said the heavyset man. "We want no trouble. The three Tibbetts boys here just want this man brought to justice."

"*Whose* justice, Marshal Weaver?" asked Case softly. "The justice of a rope flung over the nearest tree limb or a bullet in the back?"

"What's wrong with that?" asked the third of the Tibbetts men. "He killed Benny, didn't he? Benny never had a chance!"

Chet had to admit the old man had guts, standing there, almost as though we was holding off the four of them, and if Benny Tibbetts had tried to gun the major down in the street, it was a certainty that his three brothers standing there before the major with Colts at finger tip reach, could do it much easier right at that moment. The major looked directly at Chet but did not speak.

"Where is he?" demanded Charley Tibbetts.

"Right here," said Chet quietly.

The three Tibbetts men whirled as though on well oiled pivots, but they made no quick and sudden movements, not with that cold-eyed gunslinger standing there facing them in the wide doorway. They had heard how quickly Benny had received his death wound. Their eyes were as hard as agate. Weaver's eyes flicked down to the burnished star pinned to Chet's shirt. "I see," he said quietly.

"The man tried to gun the major down," said Chet quietly. "I pushed the major aside. Benny, if that was the man riding the grey, fired directly at me. I hit dirt and the bullet hit the wall right behind where my head had been. He fired at me again and missed. My last shot hit him in the back."

"*Benny* missed?" said the shortest of the three Tibbetts. "Twice? Benny Tibbetts?"

"Shut up, Harv," said Charley Tibbetts.

Marshal Weaver raised his head. "We'll have to take you back into town for questioning," he said.

"Tonight?" said Chet with a cold smile.

"Why not?" said Charley Tibbetts.

"I don't think I'd make it," said Chet.

Weaver walked forward and held out a hand. "That's not up to you."

"Stay where you are," said Chet. His voice cracked like a pistol shot.

For a long moment the marshal stood there

with his hand extended and then he dropped it. "You resisting arrest, King?" he asked.

"As sheriff of this county," said Major Case, "I'll guarantee that King is brought in tomorrow morning for any investigation that is required. Presided over by me, Marshal Weaver, not you."

Charley Tibbetts whirled. "We know what that means, Case!"

Not a muscle moved on the face of the old soldier. His eyes were without expression. "Get out of here, Tibbetts," he said quietly. "I've tolerated you long enough this night. Get out of here or I'll have my men put you off."

Another long moment of silence, then Weaver walked past Chet into the hallway. For a fraction of a second Chet thought that any one of the three Tibbetts, or all of them, might draw and shoot, but they did not. He stepped aside as they passed into the hallway. Case had handled them coolly enough. The man had sheer guts in him.

"We'll remember him, eh, Charley?" said the middle one of the three brothers.

"We'll remember him, Irv," said Charley softly.

Their booted heels rang on the paved hallway

76

and their spurs jingled musically. The door was opened for them and closed behind them by the servant girl. She managed to cast another provocative glance at Chet before she vanished somewhere within the huge, echoing house.

The major walked to an armchair and sat down. He felt along the table top until his questing fingers touched a cigar box bound in figured leather. He took out a cigar and lighted it, then shoved the box towards Chet. "Light up," he said. "I think both of us need a smoke after that to calm the nerves."

Chet selected a cigar, clipped it with the silver clipper beside the box, then lighted the fine weed. "The major didn't seem very nervous to me," he said.

"Outwardly perhaps. Those three Tibbetts men are hard case, King. Never underestimate them. The only reason Benny failed tonight was because he was drunk."

"That was how he missed me then?"

Case nodded. "I think so. I also think that he would never have attempted such a brazen shooting if he hadn't been drunk. The Tibbetts can fight any way the cards fall, King. Out in the open, sixgun flaming against sixgun, or from the dark, the rifle shot that speaks once, kills a man, and the killer vanishes."

"Nice people," said Chet. He blew a ring of smoke. "So that's the enemy?"

The major looked curiously at him. "Part of them, King. There are others. Quite a few others."

"And the stakes in this private war?"

Case waved his cigar. "That doesn't concern you . . . yet."

"A man likes to know what he is fighting for, sir."

Case smiled. "There speaks the gallant Confederate, the staunch defender of the Lost Cause."

"Why did the major fight in a blue uniform?"

Case did not answer. A log snapped in the fireplace. He leaned back in his chair. Somewhere within the great house a clock chimed nine silvery notes that echoed fleetingly through the great hallway and died away.

"Major?" asked Chet.

The grey eyes flicked at Chet. "For this," he said at last. He waved his strong hands. "This casa. The ranches. The mines. Position. Wealth. Everything I have, King, and the thought is good."

"But not for the flag, major?"

Case drew in a deep breath and looked at the end of his cigar. "That was incidental, King."

"I seem to get the idea that the major carefully picked the winning side."

Case laughed shortly. "Did you fools in gallant grey go to war for *honour*, or for slavery, King Cotton or anything else that was the old, and *profitable* way of life?"

Chet began to unpin the star from his shirt, then paused. Maybe the major was right. The days of honour and glory were long gone, as dead as the Stars and Bars, as dead as slavery and King Cotton, as dead as a man's soul can be dead when his cause is lost forever.

"Forget your honour and your glory, King," said Case harshly. "You're an American now. A private citizen of these United States whether you like it or not. Why didn't you stay in Mexico, or serve the Khedive of Egypt, or anyone else who would hire a first class mercenary such as yourself? You came back to the land you loved. You had no choice. Now you serve as a mercenary again, because you will not take the oath of allegiance. It doesn't matter to me personally. But there is a future here for you. I know. The scales are still on

your eyes. Even *I* can see better than you can."
The major laughed to himself.

Chet eyed the old man. "What are your orders, sir?" he said coldly.

"Get out of here! Idealists sicken me."

Chet walked to the door and turned to look back at the man. There was strength and courage in the old man, an irresistible drive for power within him, a cold and calculated plan for money and power, but there was something else about Bart Case that puzzled Chet. He walked out into the hallway, glancing up the long, wide staircase at the end of the hall, wondering which room was Theresa's.

He let himself out and walked slowly towards his quarters. Never before had he questioned his own decision to fight for honour, or for gold. He had considered himself a pure professional after Appomattox, and the thought that he was fighting for gold had never bothered him before.

The ranch was bathed in bright moonlight. The trees waved gracefully in the cooling wind that swept down the valley at night. The contrast between this lush valley and the harsh and naked deserts to the south was hard to believe, but death was common to both. But a man can only run so far from himself and then he must face the naked truth as he had faced the naked desert.

He had no desire to face his two companions, for a time at least. Bung had no heart in this venture, but then the big man had been slowly but steadily changing the past months. Profit was in his mind, and for that Chet could not blame him. Profit without too much danger. It was the Kid that bothered Chet. Was he serving Bart Case just to please Chet King, or because he didn't know or didn't care what kind of a situation he was getting into?

Chet took off his hat and let the night breeze cool his brow. He walked toward the *madre acequia* and stood in the shadows of the willows and cottonwoods to try and clear his teeming mind. He looked back towards the big casa and his keen eyes saw a movement in the thick shadows beneath the low ramada that bordered the south side of the house. A man and a woman stood there and his heart skipped a beat or two. Was it Theresa? He had reason to believe she thought of him as he did of her. There could only be one answer to that situation.

The soul sickness was rising within him until

the woman stepped out into the bright moon-light. It shone on her golden hair, and on the yellow hair of the lithe young man who stood hatless beside the woman. It was the Kid and Sarah Case. Trust the Kid to waste no time!

Chet shook his head. The situation was rapidly getting out of hand. He walked along the ditch, feeling the coolness of the slowly moving water rising about him. He reached the end of the trees and crossed the *acequia* by means of a narrow footbridge. He walked across a field green with growing things and stood there in the clear moonlight looking to the south where the low hills were bathed in silver light.

Chet felt for the makings and as he drew them from his shirt pocket he lost his grasp on them. He swiftly dropped his hand and bent to catch them before they struck the ground. As he did so a gun flashed amidst the tangled greenery of a bosque of trees at the far edge of the field and the bullet whispered evilly just across his bent back. He could almost feel the swift heat of its deadly passage.

Chet struck the ground and bellied towards a dry ditch as the echo of the shot fled across the sleeping valley and died away in the empty hills. A wraith of powder-smoke drifted on the dry wind. Then it was quiet again except for the rustling of the leaves.

Chet wiped the cold sweat from his face. He crawled along the ditch with ready Colt in his hands, taking his time, peering every now and again at the silent bosque ahead of him. There was no sight nor sound of anyone in there. He looked back at the house. The sound of excited voices came to him from the vicinity of the big casa and the other ranch buildings.

Half an hour drifted past before he reached the edge of the bosque. He eased himself up beside a tree and peered into the moonlighted bosque. It was empty. On all sides of it were the wide fields. Chet walked softly into the trees. The moonlight shone on an empty cartridge case. He picked it up and sniffed it, noting the sharp, acrid odour of freshly burned powder. Half a dozen cigarette butts littered the ground. He looked toward the place where he had been standing. The area was bathed in clear light. It had hardly been possible for even an average shot to miss in that light and at that range.

Whoever had been there had been waiting for some time, if the cigarette butts indicated the passage of time like a silent clock. Maybe there had been more than one man. He looked about again. The soft earth clearly indicated tracks heading for the south side of the bosque, away from the direction of the ranch buildings. The bushwhacker was long gone by now.

Chet shrugged. He left the grove and walked slowly across the wide field, with an intolerable itching between his shoulder blades. It wasn't likely that the Tibbetts men had done the job, for whoever had been waiting there had been there long before the Tibbetts men had left the casa. Chet looked back at the bosque. Only his act in stooping for the falling tobacco had saved his life. Cold sweat trickled down his sides. "I'm getting too damned old for this sort of thing," he growled to himself. He rolled the cigarette he had wanted half an hour before and walked slowly and thoughtfully to the quarters.

Bung was sound asleep in his bunk, mouth agape, breath harsh and regular, empty bottle lying on the floor beside his hand. Chet found another bottle and drank deeply. He felt the warmth and soporific effect of the liquor take hold almost at once. He pulled off his boots, doused the lamp, then lay flat on his cot staring up at the whitewashed ceiling.

He was still awake when the Kid came

quietly into the room, pulled off his boots, trousers and shirt, then scaled his hat at a wall hook. The hat struck the hook, swung uneasily back and forth, then settled for the night. The Kid grinned as he got into bed.

The Kid was fast asleep when Chet got up. He walked to the door and barred it. He peered through a window toward the big casa. One yellow lighted window showed on the second floor. Sarah's room without doubt. Then the light flicked out. He padded across the room and peered across the irrigation ditch toward the bosque where the hidden marksman had waited for him. The moon was almost gone. The fields and the bosque were as quiet as the grave. He shivered a little at the simile.

He got back into bed and lay for a long time staring at the ceiling, but thinking not of the hard-eyed Tibbetts men, or the man who had tried to kill him that night, but rather of the soft, clinging, honeysweet mouth of Theresa Case.

6

THE afternoon sun was beating down into the plaza of Two Rivers. It was siesta time, for those who could afford a siesta, but Two Rivers wasn't asleep. Not with the undercurrent of excitement and latent danger that overhung the otherwise sleepy town. The group of men who were in the sheriff's big office had been in there for a long time, and at any minute the top might blow off the office in a wild burst of gunfire if the raging anger of the Tibbetts men broke loose like a feral beast to rend and slay.

Bart Case had listened quietly to the accusations of the Tibbetts men. All the time the accusations were hurled, the stranger from Texas, the tall, hard-eyed man named Chet King, who wore a deputy's star on his shirt, leaned easily against the wall near the closed window, watching the taut faces of Charley, Irv and Harv Tibbetts, and that of Town Marshal Holt Weaver. There were no other Case men in the smoke filled room, but lounging outside on the street before the sheriff's building were the two men who had ridden into Two Rivers just the day before. The big man incongruously nicknamed Bung, and the slim, cold-eyed youth nicknamed the Kid. There were other men lounging about the sun washed *placita* and everyone in Two Rivers could tell you which of them were Case men and which were Tibbetts men. There were a lot of them.

"You've got no way of proving that Benny shot first," said Holt Weaver. "I said that before and I'll say it again."

Chet began to roll a cigarette. That morning, riding into Two Rivers, Bart Case had told him of the struggle for power in the valley of the Two Rivers. It wasn't a new situation. Townsmen against rancher was an old struggle in the Southwest. It was really more than that though, for the Tibbetts men were ranchers as well as Bart Case. It was Case's hands on the check reins of the area that really bothered the Tibbetts clan. Bart Case had lived in New Mexico since the days of the American Occupation, after coming to the Territory as a volunteer under Doniphan. He had seen the great possibilities of Two Rivers, had taken every cent he could scrape, beg and borrow, to invest in Two Rivers land. He had been voted into the Territorial Legislature before the war. Though he had not mentioned buying votes, or telling his employees and renters to vote for him, or else, there wasn't any doubt in Chet's mind that Case had used such a time honored method.

Later on, during the war, Case had formed a battalion of militia from Two Rivers men, and had served in the First New Mexico under Kit Carson, with honour. There was nothing that Bart Case had missed in his steady and relentless climb to power in his chosen bailiwick. He had achieved his sheriffship the same way that he had achieved his political goals before the war. In new Mexico of the post war years, a sheriff could wield almost feudal power if he so desired, and Bart Case had so desired.

Chet eyed Case. Some of the man's methods irritated him, but then the Tibbetts men were no better. It was a case of dog in the manger as far as Case was concerned, and he was a tough, infighting hound when the chips were down. Nothing spared and nothing barred until the loser went battling to the floor and died in a welter of blood.

Bart Case listened to the hot and angry words

of his enemies, then leaned back in his chair. "Vincente!" he called.

A little man came into the room from the corridor that led to the cells. Behind him was the man named Mark Stoughton. Vincente looked back over his shoulder into the face of the jailkeeper, and what he saw there was enough to make him change his mind about making a break for the street. He was badly frightened.

Bart Case looked at the little man. "Vincente Casias," he said quietly. "Tell these men what you saw in the street last night after dusk."

A drop of sweat rolled from the man's forehead. He wet his lips and swallowed hard.

"Go on, Vincente," said the sheriff.

"Major Case and the tall man there, against the wall, were starting to cross the street," blurted out Vincente. He saw the looks from the Tibbetts men and his voice dragged to a halt.

"Go on!" snapped Case.

The little man was between the devil and the deep blue sea, damned if he talked and damned if he didn't. "A man came at them, riding a grey horse, and he had a pistola in his hand . . ." Vincente closed his eyes and crossed himself. "The tall man over there pushed the major back against the wall and dropped to the ground."

"What tall man?" said Case. "Point him out, man!"

Vincente's dirty forefinger indicated Chet. "The man on the horse fired at the tall man but he had dropped to the ground. The man on the ground fired his pistola and missed. The man on the horse fired again. His bullet struck the earth not far from the tall man there. The tall man fired once more. I did not see the bullet strike the man on the horse. He rode swiftly away into the darkness . . ."

"Who was that horseman, Vincente?" demanded Case.

"It was the man known as Benny Tibbetts!" blurted out Vincente. He stopped talking as though someone had cut his throat. His eyes widened as he saw the looks on the faces of the Tibbetts men. He crossed himself again. "May I go back to my cell now, patron?" he asked Case.

Bart Case leaned back in his chair. "Well, Weaver," he said quietly.

"Where did you find *him?*" said the marshal. He jerked a thumb at Vincente Casias.

"I work for the patron," babbled Vincente.

"You sure do," said Charley Tibbetts. He walked to the door and turned. He smiled, but there was no mirth on his death mask of a face. "Stay locked up in that cell, *Mister* Casias," he said softly. "Don't walk any dark streets at night, *Mister* Casias."

"Don't intimidate the witness," said Bart Case.

Charley Tibbetts walked out, followed by his two brothers.

Holt Weaver eyed Case. "Very neat, Major Case," he said.

"Are you accusing Vincente Casias of being a false witness?" said Case coolly.

Weaver shrugged. "It's no longer my affair," he said.

Case leaned forward and looked directly at the marshal. "You've lined yourself up with the Tibbetts bunch for sure now, Weaver. I'll give you a chance to redeem yourself with me. Either you back me up in Two Rivers, Weaver, or you back them up. Which is it to be?"

Weaver shifted his gaze. He looked at Chet King and gained little comfort in what he saw.

"There is no neutral ground, Weaver," continued Case.

"And if I back you, I keep the job, is that it, Case?"

"*Major* Case," said the sheriff.

"Major then!" snapped the marshal.

"Think it over, Weaver," said Case.

Weaver jammed his hat on his head and stomped from the office. Case lighted a cigar. He laughed softly. "I wonder if he's more scared of me than the Tibbetts clan?"

"No neutral ground," said Chet quietly. He eyed the sheriff. "There was no witness in that street last night."

Case looked up at him through a cloud of smoke. "He told it the way it happened, didn't he?"

"He had to, didn't he?"

Case leaned forward and took the cigar from his mouth. "This is war, King, and no holds barred. I can't afford to have you up for a murder trial. I have other plans for you."

"And Vincente Casias?"

Case waved a hand. "He'll be well paid. If he wants to leave the country I can see to that too."

"Supposing they get to him first?"

Case smiled thinly. "He'll have a damned fine funeral, King."

The man had a shell like a tortoise, thought Chet. "The plaza is full of Tibbetts men," he said.

"There are a lot of my men out there too, King."

Chet looked from the window. Bung and the Kid were leaning against a tree in front of the building. Here and there beneath the shade of other trees were men standing there, quietly smoking, waiting for something. Just waiting . . . One spark and the whole placita would go up like a blown powder magazine.

Case relighted his cigar. "On the other side of the valley there is a man named Frank Miles. He has a small spread. I happen to have a dispossession notice against him. It was dated three days ago. Miles is still at the ranch. Go on out there and get him off that land." Case handed a folded paper to Chet. "There's your authority. If he resists, arrest him and bring him in."

"Do you think he will?"

Case shrugged. "Miles is a hard man, King. He might."

"Shall I go alone?"

"Take a couple of men."

"Who?"

Case waved a hand. "Bring in your two friends. I'll swear them in temporarily." He looked up at Chet. "Get Miles off that land by dusk tonight."

Twenty minutes later Chet and his two companeros were riding out in the valley road. There had been no trouble in the streets of Two Rivers, but there were men standing in the bars who were talking a little ugly about the killing of Benny Tibbetts. Still none of them were overly anxious to accost Chet King, particularly when he was sided by two of his amigos. There was plenty of time and a man couldn't always be on his guard.

Clouds raced after their shadows across the wide valley. The wind was soft. The valley was quiet and peaceful, but still at the back of Chet's mind there was that constant uneasiness.

"Possemen," said Bung. "What next?"

The Kid grinned. "Chet said we ought'a stay on the right side of the law for a change."

Bung glanced sideways at Chet. For years he had always been close to Chet King, but seemingly, ever since that hot little fracas at Hueco Tanks, the tall man had been more withdrawn than Bung had ever remembered seeing him. It was the tall, dark girl, thought Bung. If

94

anything broke up the three of them it would be a woman. It was always that way. The Kid was young. He could adapt himself and he had his blue eyes on the younger filly, the one with the cornsilk hair. She'd take care of the kid, and the tall, dark one had been the lure for Chet King. That left ol' Bungo, and ol' Bungo was beginning to wonder just where *he* fitted in.

The Miles place was tucked into a far corner of the valley, and was cut up by arroyos and great paws of rock and earth that thrust themselves out from the surrounding hills. It was a small place, but the land seemed good and there was plenty of water. Smoke rose from the adobe house that was set between two of the hill spurs. Cattle lowed from near the stream. A windmill whirred in the wind.

"Not bad," said Bung. He rubbed his bristly jaws. "What did this hombre do to get kicked off his place?"

"*Quien sabe?*" said Chet. "I didn't ask any questions."

"You're changing, Chet," said the Kid.

Chet shot a hard glance at him, but the Kid did not look away, and something in the Kid's

95

eyes told Chet that he had spoken nothing but the truth.

They dismounted near the gate and walked toward the house, leading their horses. Chet was in the lead. There was no one in sight. He was within fifty feet of the front of the house when the rifle barrel poked out of a window. "Stay where you are!" said a woman's voice.

Chet smiled. "I'm here to see Mister Frank Miles," he said.

"On what business?" she asked.

She sounded young, but Chet couldn't see her. "The sheriff sent me out, ma'am. I have a dispossess notice for Mister Miles."

There was a long silence. The rifle barrel did not move. Then she spoke again. "The major never gives up, does he?"

Chet shrugged. "I wouldn't know anything about that."

"You're new on the job then?"

"Yes," admitted Chet, "but that doesn't mean I don't intend to carry the major's orders through."

She laughed. "You're all alike."

Chet moved a little closer to the house. "Put down that rifle," he said. "I came to see Frank

Miles, not some hidden female with a rifle in her hands."

"My father can't see anyone right now, mister."

Chet glanced back at his two companions. The Kid was grinning. "You goin' to charge them *breastworks*, Chet? Haw!"

Chet looked about. The place seemed deserted. "Is Mister Miles on the premises?" he asked.

"Yes."

"Then I am going to see him."

"No!" she snapped.

Chet eyed the unmoving rifle barrel. "Listen, ma'am," he said quietly. "This is the law speaking. For the last time, put down that rifle and tell me where I can find Mister Miles."

"Law?" she said. "Law? The personal law of *Major* Bart Case! He'll tell you one thing and do another! He had no right to send you out here. His word doesn't mean a thing does it?"

Chet reached for the makings. It wasn't like him to chivvy a female, especially an angry one with a loaded Spencer repeater in her hands. "Look," he said at last, "if I put down my gun, can I see him?"

"What about the other two?"

"I'll send them back to the road."

In the quietness that followed Chet could hear the low murmuring of voices from the house. "All right," she called out.

Chet jerked his head at his two companions. They led their horses back to the road, through the gate, then squatted in the shade of the trees eyeing Chet curiously while they rolled cigarettes. Chet unbuckled his gunbelt and let it drop to the ground. The front door of the house swung open. He stepped up onto the porch and walked into the dark, cool interior of the house.

"He's in the bedroom," she said.

Chet glanced at her. She stood in a corner, still in darkness, and the rifle was in her slim hands. He walked to the bedroom and saw a lean, gaunt faced man propped up in the big bed. Pain wracked eyes studied Chet. "Another one?" said the man in the bed. "The pattern never changes. Seems like Bart Case gets all his deputies from the same mould."

Chet's eyes narrowed. "The name is King," he said.

"Texas man?"

Chet nodded.

Miles shifted a little. "So am I," he said.

"I thought so," said Chet. "Smoke, Mister Miles?"

Miles shook his head. "Bothers my chest," he said. He studied Chet. "Is it that damned dispossess notice again?"

"Yes."

"Bart Case told me I could have an extension on my note."

"Who has the note?"

Miles smiled faintly. "Bart Case." He looked up at Chet. "The sheriff sends out a man to dispossess me from land I bought from a rancher, because I couldn't pay off a note from the banker."

"So?"

Miles raised his right hand and let it drop on the counterpane. "Sheriff Case and Rancher Case and Banker Case."

Chet leaned against the wall. "Nothing illegal about that, is there?"

"Not really." Miles jerked his head at a chair. "Sit down," he said. "Nancy!" he called out. "Bring Mister King a cup of coffee, or whatever he likes."

"Let him get it himself," she said coldly.

Chet turned with a faint smile to look at her. She was the feisty one all right. His eyes widened despite himself. She was in her early twenties, brown haired and tanned of skin, a rarity amongst the fashionable set of ranch women, if they could possibly avoid it. It was her eyes that caught Chet's full interest. They were a shade of green he had never seen, seemingly flecked with gold, like the brown eyes of Theresa Case.

"Seen enough, mister?" she said quietly.

Chet grinned. "No," he said, "but I came to see your Paw, not you, Miss Nancy."

She turned on a booted heel and left the room, leaving Chet King with a firm memory of svelte, lean flanks, covered with blue jean material. Lithe in the flanks, and slim in the pasterns. One of the finest human mares Chet had seen since he had crossed the Rio Grande *this* trip anyway.

"Nancy is spunky," said Frank Miles.

Chet flipped his cigarette butt into the garboon beside the bed and rolled another. "I hate to kick a sick man out into the road, Mister Miles," he said, "but I don't see how I can get around it. Is there any way you can talk to Major Case?"

"With a double-barrelled shotgun in my

hands," said Miles grimly. "He just might understand that."

"I doubt it," said Chet.

"How come a Texas man is linked up with that Yankee?"

Chet smiled. "He needed real fighting men," he said.

"You're a Texan all right," said Miles. "No, there is no way I can reason with Bart Case. I made the mistake of taking his word. Where *I* come from in Texas, a man's word is his bond."

"Hear, hear," said Chet quietly. He lighted the cigarette.

Miles closed his eyes. "I would have made it all right," he said, "except for this wound."

"Wound?"

Miles nodded. "Happened about a month ago. I was on Case's range, looking for strays. Some bushwhacker fired at me from a bosque on the other side of the river. Bullet hit me high on the left shoulder. I've been hit harder than that in the war, but I got a touch of something along with the wound and it isn't healing too well. Nothing I could do. Nancy kept the place going. She went in to see Bart Case but he wouldn't even talk with her. I had to let some

101

of my vaqueros go. Couldn't pay them. Nancy sold my cows for what she could get."

"To Bart Case?"

Miles opened his eyes. "Well, he picked through the herd, took the best and paid the least. I've got no income from this place, King."

"How much is the note?"

"One thousand dollars."

"Hardly pay for the buildings, would it?"

Miles shook his head. "The spread is small, but it's a good one, King. Fine location. Plenty of water. Sheltered from winter winds. Well, there ain't no use in talking about it." Miles shifted again and it was then that Chet noticed the left sleeve of the flannel nightgown was empty.

Chet stood up. "What regiment were you with, Miles?"

"Terry's Texas Rangers."

Chet stared at him. "They were part of Wharton's division at Chickamauga. I was there with the Eleventh Texas, *mister*. I never saw you there."

Miles shook his head. "Lost my arm long before that, *mister*. At Shiloh."

"Sorry, Miles."

The man smiled. "You didn't know." He eyed Chet. "How much time do I have?"

"The notice was dated three days ago."

Miles closed his eyes again.

Chet walked to the door. "I'll send out a doctor, Miles. If he says you can't be moved, you stay here until you can move."

"Gracias, King."

Chet walked to the front door. Nancy was standing on the porch. She looked at him. "That was nice of you," she said a little stiffly.

"Case can hardly drive him from the place if he's not able to go."

"You don't know your *patron* very well, Mister King."

Chet did not answer. She was right. He didn't know Bart Case very well at that. "Would he take his payment now?" he said quietly.

"I doubt it," she said. She shrugged. "Besides, we haven't got it."

"No place to get it either?"

"No one in Two Rivers would loan Dad the money. They're all afraid of Bart Case. There isn't time to go anywhere else for the money." She smiled wryly. "There isn't anyone we know anywhere who would loan us that kind of money."

He picked up his gunbelt and smiled. "All right to put this on?" he asked.

She nodded. "It was foolish of me to hold you off like that."

"I might have done the same thing," he said.

"You're a strange one for a Case man."

He eyed her. "I hardly knew Bart Case when he deputized me."

"How did he happen to hire you? Through reputation?"

"In a way."

Her eyes narrowed. "You must be the man who saved Theresa and Sarah Case down in Texas!"

"Yes."

"I have a feeling you'll be back," she said quietly. "This time your heart won't let you allow Dad to get off the hook. That will be seen to."

"By Bart Case?"

She tilted her head to one side and studied him. "One of the Cases," she said enigmatically. "Good day, Mister King." She walked back into the house.

Chet buckled his gunbelt about his lean hips

and walked to his horse. He mounted it and rode slowly toward the gate. He turned as he reached the gate to see her face framed in the window. She disappeared as he looked at her.

"Well," said Bung. "What about it?"

Chet rolled another cigarette. "Frank Miles was with Terry's Texas Rangers at Shiloh."

"So?"

"Lost his left arm there."

"Too bad!" Bung picked at his yellow teeth with a fingernail. He eyed Chet speculatively. "Now, a man like you, Chet, deputized by the major, ain't going to let that fact stop him from doing his bound and lawful duty, is it?"

Chet lighted the cigarette.

Bung grinned. "Or is it that little filly who did the trick?"

Chet took the cigarette from his mouth. "Sometimes, Mister Burkbennett, you talk just too goddamned much!"

Bung flushed. His whole body seemed to bristle. "Don't you talk that way to me, Mister King!"

"Take it easy, *amigos*," said the Kid.

Chet kneed his horse away from them. "Go on back to town. Tell Case I had to stay here.

Tell him anything. Just keep him quiet until I can talk to him."

Bung looked down at the star pinned to his cowhide vest. "First and last time I'll ever wear one of these goddamned Judas things!" He swung up into his saddle with a smashing of leather and spurred his horse toward town.

The Kid shrugged. He mounted and looked at Chet. "The major ain't goin' to take any excuses from you, Chet."

"He will," said Chet.

"Things ain't quite going the way you figured they would are they?"

"I just told Mister Bungo Burkbennett that he talked too much."

The Kid smiled thinly. He held up a hand. "All right, Chet. But it was your idea to come up here and go to work for Case. Like Bungo said: 'Sold your birthright for a mess of pottage, like it says in the Good Book'."

Chet's face whitened. "When you talk like that to me Kid, you'd better make sure you're the man you think you are."

It was the Kid's turn to whiten. "I can take care of myself, Chet. Thanks to you. You taught me all I know. *Buenos tardes*, Chet." He raked his horse with his spurs and slammed down the road after the retreating figure of Bung Burkbennett.

Chet sat his horse in the middle of the sunny road for a few minutes, then he turned it and rode the other way toward the distant pink and salmon coloured hills, stippled with pinons like cloves stuck in gigantic hams. A man had to have time to think and events had been piling too swiftly, one atop another, for a man to sort them out and evaluate them, and at such a time, for a man like Chet King, at least, he must find his answer in the solitudes. The solitudes of the empty hills, where God sometimes speaks to the receptive.

7

THE big casa on the Case rancho stood out through the velvety darkness, the rectangles and squares of yellow lamplight sharp and clear. The wind swayed the great trees in a steady and pleasing rustling. A mule bawled from a corral. The windmill whirred, slowed down, turned slowly, began to whirr again, then picked up speed into a steady thrumming sound that played the counter melody to the rustling of the trees.

Chet King reined in his horse on the ridge to the east of the great rancho. The wide valley of the Two Rivers seemed to be dozing in the thick pre-moon darkness. A scarf of smoke lay low over the river and was being ravelled out by the rising wind. Far to the south was the rancho of Frank Miles, hidden behind the great spurs of the rough hills. Beyond the Case rancho, to the west, huddled against the western limits of the valley was the irregular cluster of lights that was the town of Two Rivers.

Chet rolled a cigarette and placed it, unlighted between his lips. He had suddenly remembered the shot from the darkness that could easily have killed him. He threw down the cigarette and satisfied himself with a chew of tobacco. There was an uneasiness within him. He had not been able to get rid of it all that day after he had left the rancho of Frank Miles. Time and time again the grave eyes of Nancy Miles had seemed to dominate his restless thoughts and when it wasn't the eyes of Nancy Miles that bothered it, it was the great, gold flecked eyes of Theresa Case. "Like a sick pup," he said angrily to the warm night wind.

He touched the horse with his heels and rode down toward the range road that would lead him to the ranch buildings. He drew his Winchester and loaded the chamber, riding with the weapon across his thighs. He only wanted to see one person at that time. Bart Case. He had no idea of what Bung and the Kid had told the major, or whether or not Case had accepted what they had told him. If he had not, then Chet might be riding into a situation from which he might not easily escape. Case had asked but two things from his employees. Loyalty and fighting ability when he needed.

That and no more, although always in the back of Chet's mind there had been the thought that Case wanted more from Chet. Nothing that a man could put his finger upon, but it was there all the same. He had also said something else: *"I never forget men who serve me. Never . . ."* A man could take that two ways, and one of them would not be pleasant.

It would be easy enough for Chet to pull out. To ride across the dark hills. To vanish from the troubles and bloodshed of the Valley of the Two Rivers.

He had reached the white painted rock wall that separated the area of the ranch buildings from the grazing land between it and the river. Something moved amidst the swaying trees. Trust Bart Case to have his stronghold well guarded.

"Quien es?" called out a vaguely familiar voice.

"Chet King," said Chet. He moved his rifle a little.

A man moved out from the trees. It was the one named Santiago, who had first guided, or escorted Chet and his two companeros to Jose Silva.

The man nodded. "I have been watching

you," he said casually. He began to roll a cigarette.

Chet eyed the guards. "Are my two friends here?" he asked.

"The big one and the muchacho? Si. They are somewhere around. At least I think they are."

Chet dismounted and led the horse through the gateway as Santiago opened it, watching the man all the time. The vaquero smiled. "I see you carry your rifle handy," he said. "That is well."

Chet eyed him. "Why so, amigo?"

Santiago shrugged. "We who work for Major Case are often targets for others. It is part of the business."

"Yes," said Chet drily. "Part of the business." He led his horse toward the buildings, followed by the dark and speculative eyes of the vaquero.

Chet emptied the chamber of his Winchester, scabbarded it, then tethered the horse to a tree near the big casa. The place was quiet. It was almost too quiet to suit him. No one appeared as he walked toward the large double doors that were the main entrance into the house. He tapped on the door. No one answered. He tried

the door and it swung open easily on its great
noiseless hinges. The hall was empty of life.
There was no one in the living room though a
fire leaped and danced on the hearth. Chet
walked on into the paved hallway. The dining
room was dark and empty. The cooking was
done in a separate building at the rear of a
vegetable garden between it and the house.

Chet looked up the broad staircase. Bart Case
had built well. The place was as sumptuous and
large as many of the great Mexican ranchos he
had seen, and in the days after the war, he had
helped to loot as well, until the gringo mercenaries had been forced to flee back across the
border. He walked quietly up the stairs. At the
front of the second floor a door was ajar and he
could see lamplight. He walked to the doorway
and tapped on it.

"Who is it?" asked Major Case.

"Chet King, Major Case."

There was a pause. "Come in then," said the
rancher.

Chet opened the door. Case stood near the
wide window looking between the tall trees
towards the distant, twinkling lights of Two
Rivers. He did not turn. "Where have you
been, King?" he asked at last.

"I went out to the Miles place as you ordered."

The major cut a hand sideways. "I know that," he said quickly. "Where have you been since then?"

"Riding."

"That's one hell of an answer to give your boss," said Case harshly.

"It's one hell of a way to talk to a man," said Chet quietly. "You can at least face me, major."

The erect back stiffened. Case turned. The room was lighted only by an Argand desk lamp which threw its pool of yellow light on top of the polished desk and the white papers thereon. Chet could hardly see the major's face, but he could guess at the expression on it.

Chet walked toward the desk. "I went out to the Miles place," he said. "I can't say that I liked the thought of kicking a very sick man from his bed."

"That was no concern of yours."

"Perhaps," admitted Chet.

"Then why didn't you do it?"

Chet could feel the powerful will of the man striking at him through the lamplight. Bart Case had not risen to his position in life by accepting weak excuses, or any excuses at all from his subordinates. "I didn't accept this job with the knowledge that I would have to dispossess invalids from their beds," said Chet.

Case again cut his hand sideways. "You accepted the job without any other conditions than that I expected loyalty, and fighting ability from you, and that goes for *any* of my *employees*."

The sneering tone of the man cut like a whip-lash. Chet moved closer to the desk. He didn't want to get involved in an argument about the dubious ethics of Major Bart Case, as compared to his own rather shady ethics.

"I don't usually listen to excuses," said the major.

"Maybe I don't intend to give any," said Chet.

Case stared at him. "Then why did you come back at all?" he asked.

"Frank Miles owes you one thousand dollars on a note. Is that correct?"

Case nodded.

"You granted him an extension on that note."

Case waved a hand. "Verbally," he said.

"Your word is not good then?"

Case leaned forward and placed his hands flat

on the desk. "You sound like a damned shyster lawyer," he said coldly. "The note was due. It wasn't paid. Whatever I said to Frank Miles doesn't have anything to do with you, King. Now get out to the Miles place. Now! Get that man off of that property before dawn, or by God, King, I'll. . . ." His voice trailed off. He looked at Chet with a fixed gaze, a great vein throbbed in his left temple, and it looked as though he was going to leap at Chet to rend and tear like a beast of the jungle.

Chet slid his hand inside his jacket and withdrew his wallet. He opened the worn leather and slowly counted out ten one hundred dollar bills. He placed them on the desk between the hands of the rancher. "There's the one thousand dollars due on the note," he said quietly.

For a moment Case stared at Chet. "Did Frank Miles pay you that money?"

"Yes."

"You're lying to me, King."

"One thousand dollars is due. One thousand dollars lies on your desk. Now give me a receipt and let Frank Miles live on his ranch in peace."

It was then that Chet King had the feeling that the two of them were not alone in that big room. It ran the entire width of the house, but at the south end, a partition had been built, probably to shield a bed from the rest of the room. Chet glanced out of the corners of his eyes. The partitioned end of the room was thick in shadow. The moon had not yet risen to shed its light into the windows. Chet stepped back a little.

"Take this damned money back to where you got it," said Case coldly.

"No," said Chet. He moved closer to the door, watching that partition but keeping an eye on the major as well. "You make out a receipt for that one thousand dollars, major."

"No."

"It's legal enough, isn't it?"

"Damn you and your legality! When I gave you that star, King, I expected a man who would do as he was told! Not a carping idiot who pays off bills for shiftless no account Texans!"

"Take it easy," said Chet softly. "The money is there, Case. Now give me that receipt."

"I refuse."

In the pause that followed the major's refusal, Chet heard a soft step in the hall outside of the major's room. Maybe the net was closing in. No

116

wonder it had been so easy to approach the house and enter it without interference.

Chet stepped back against the wall and drew his Colt. The hammer snicked back. "Sign," said he quietly.

Case had no expression on his face. "You draw on *me?*" he said incredulously. "Sheriff of this county? In my own home? You, a damned ragtag, unreconstructed rebel? Why, damn you to hell, King!"

"Sign," said Chet. "If any of your men interfere, the first bullet is for you."

Case laughed shortly. "I've faced guns before," he said.

"Sign!"

Case sat down. His face was still in semi-darkness. He took a piece of paper and dipped pen in ink. He wrote steadily in a loose sort of a scrawl. He signed the receipt. Chet walked to the desk and read it. It was valid enough. He unpinned the star from his shirt and placed it in the yellow pool of light and the touch of the metal seemed almost to sicken him. There was no movement from Bart Case for a moment, then his left hand crept out to close over the star. He was looking directly at Chet, and although his face was hidden in the darkness beyond the lamplight, Chet could almost feel the hatred that had formed on it.

"How far do you think you'll get with that receipt?" said Case.

"What's a thousand dollars to you?" said Chet. "Is it worthwhile to kill a man over a little thing like this?"

Case swept the money from the desk. It fluttered noiselessly to the carpeted floor.

"It wasn't the money at all, was it, Case?" said Chet.

"*Major* Case!"

"No Yankee major can make me call him that," said Chet coldly. "You wanted the whole thing, didn't you? The Miles place was your goal, not the payment of a due note. Why, Case? Haven't you got *enough?*"

"Get out," said the rancher.

Chet backed to beside the door. "I said the first bullet was for you, Case."

The rancher laughed harshly. "What do you want? Free passage? All I have to do is call out and you'll get shot to doll rags."

"After you," said Chet.

The hands tightened and formed into fists. "I said I had faced guns before, King."

The man could not be bluffed. His ego wouldn't let him quail before Chet.

Chet eyed the door. He caught the faint, dry sound of breathing on the other side of it. He stepped quickly towards the door, then smashed it hard with a shoulder, driving it fully open, to leap out into the hallway, thrusting his Colt hard into the belly of the man who stood there. Jose Silva's eyes widened. Chet plucked the rifle from the man's hands and stepped back. "Get in there," he said, jerking his head toward the room. He saw the look of pure hate on the man's dark face as he looked back over his shoulder. Chet pulled the door shut behind Silva, then looked along the hallway. His ears caught the sound of low voices coming from the stair well. He padded along the right hand side of the well. At the end of the hall he stopped and looked back. He could hear Case's raging voice.

The first floor was too dangerous for Chet. He looked about. Behind him was a deepset doorway. He tried the door. It swung open easily. He stepped inside and closed it, turning the key in the lock. The faint odour of perfume came to him, mingled with a purely feminine aura. He turned quickly.

Theresa Case was standing in the middle of the room, clad in a filmy negligee with her thick dark hair flowing over her bare white shoulders. The moon was rising beyond the valley and there was enough light for Chet to see the silhouette of her long, beautiful legs through the sheer material. He raised his eyes to look at her.

"What have you done?" she said.

"Your father and I had a little disagreement," he said quietly.

She tilted her lovely head to one side and studied him. "You're running then?" She looked at the rifle and pistol in his hands.

He smiled thinly. "I don't think your father exactly wants to let me go without a struggle."

"Why?"

"I paid off the Miles debt. He refused to sign a receipt for it. I made him do it."

She stared at him. "You made my father sign a receipt? I've never heard of *anyone* making him do a thing like that."

"He did," said Chet drily.

He heard booted feet on the staircase. He leaned the rifle against the wall and closed in on her, placing a hand across her full, soft mouth. "Keep quiet," he said. Her breasts pressed firmly against his arm. Her great eyes studied him above his clasping hand.

They were in the hallway now. A door banged open and the major's voice came clearly to Chet. "Get that sonofabitch of a Texan! Jose! Round up the boys! Adolfo! Search the house! Nick! Take some men and go find those two companeros of his! Move, damn you! Pronto! *Andele! Andele!*"

She was so close he could feel the warmth emanating from her body. "If I take my hand from your mouth," he whispered, "will you be quiet?"

She nodded. As he removed his hand she pressed closer to him and held up her mouth invitingly. It was hardly the time and place, but Chet King took the time to kiss her. He walked to the open window and looked down into the garden. Men were moving about in the shadows. The moon had not yet lighted the grounds.

"You're a fool, Chet," she said quietly.

He turned to look at her. "I can't do his kind of work, Theresa," he said.

"How do you think he got where he is?"

"I have a good idea," he said drily.

"This is a hard country, Chet. The weak ones

fall. The fighters either die or join men like my father."

"He can't go on forever," he said.

She hesitated. "No, Chet. That is why I talked him into taking you on as his deputy, sight unseen."

He walked to the door and placed his ear against it. The hallway was quiet. He turned and looked at her. "Go on," he said in a low voice.

"Don't you see, Chet?" she said quickly. "He's getting along in years. He still holds his men and his position because of his past, but he has been slipping. If he had had a son, or sons to take over, it would have been perfect."

Chet tilted his head to one side and studied her. "But he got a daughter instead."

She smiled and came close to him. "Yes, I do what I can to make up for being a female. Chet."

"You do all right," he said. He looked down at her lush body. "Never be ashamed of being a woman, Theresa."

"It isn't that," she said. "I'm glad that I am a woman. I'm glad that I can bring a man to take my father's place. Not a son perhaps, but a son-in-law who can take the reins and run this valley as he had done. My *husband*, Chet."

He half closed his eyes. Her nearness to him was a fearful temptation, but his feeling for her would keep him from doing what his unbridled passions would have forced him to do. He wanted Theresa Case. God how he wanted her! There was nothing he had to give her but his love. She was beautiful and young; passionate and warm; she had brains with her beauty, and position and wealth enough to look forward to a future of success, and happiness too, if she did not let her father's example lead her astray.

"Do you understand me, Chet?" she said softly.

He smiled. "I think I've upset the applecart already," he said.

"Don't you want me, Chet?"

"God yes!" He drew her close and showed her by his lips and questing hands how much he wanted her. Under different circumstances he knew he'd never be able to hold his desire in check. It was difficult enough as it was.

Her lips clung to his, then parted reluctantly. She cupped his lean, hawk's face in her slim, soft hands. "Then don't worry about him," she whispered. "I can straighten things out, Chet. He'll listen to me. He has to listen to me."

"He listens to no one," he said grimly.

She pressed his face tightly in her hands. "He *has* to listen to me, Chet," she said. Her negligee fell from a lovely white shoulder and revealed the upper curve of her left breast, almost to the tip of it. He remembered those buds on the full breasts as he had seen them that dawn at Hueco Tanks, and the rest of her long legged nakedness as well, as she lay on the ground beneath the Apache, an instant before violation. "He must listen. He can't go on much longer," she continued.

Chet eyed her. Forgotten were her physical charms. There was something diamond hard about this lovely creature; something beneath the exquisitely moulded feminity of her. "What do you mean?" he asked.

"He has to pass on his power to someone, Chet. His wealth goes to me and my husband. A husband who can be as strong as he was. A man who can keep the reins in his hands, as my father did."

"He's doing all right," he said quietly.

"Let me go to him," she said. "I'll straighten things out. Stay here!"

"Wait," he said. "What are you driving at, Theresa?"

She searched his face. "Don't you understand what I am offering you?"

"I'm not sure."

She turned away from him and her negligee, either accidentally, or through intent, fell from her smooth white shoulders, to hang from the thin cord that bound it about her waist. She made no effort to raise it, or cover herself with her arms. She turned slowly and faced him, then gripped his wrists in a strength that surprised him, as she drew him towards the wide bed. She fell backward on the bed and drew on his wrists. "Now Chet," she whispered hoarsely, "now, before I change my mind, before I realize what I am doing!"

It was hell for Chet King. He stood there staring at her lushness and her parted lips, her devouring eyes, and, perversely, he knew he wanted no part of this woman, either for a night's passionate dalliance, or through the rest of his life. She had sickened him as she had once intrigued him, and the extremes were like the poles apart.

"Chet!" she said. Her eyes widened. "I can

get you back in his graces! All of this can be ours and we'll have our love as well."

He stepped back. She was the daughter of her father all right.

"Chet?" She sat up and stared almost wildly at him. Her naked breasts rose and fell. A crystal droplet of sweat coursed from her chest and ran for cover in the deep cleft of her bosom.

He stepped back a little further.

"Chet!" she snapped. Then she was on her feet, driving toward him, completely oblivious of her half nakedness. Her nails clawed at his face and drew blood while her slippered feet hammered at his shins. Incongruously enough he remembered Hueco Tanks again and of how she had fought silently and desperately against the Apache buck until he had hurled her soft, tender flesh against the harsh abrasion of the desert floor.

Then she opened her mouth to scream, and as the full lips were squared, a fraction of a second before she could give voice, his left fist caught her neatly on the side of the jaw, and she fell silently back on the bed, bounced and rolled over onto the floor to lie still.

He picked up the rifle and walked to the window. There was a balcony beyond it, shaded

126

by vines that hung from the wide tile eaves of the house. He stepped out onto it and saw a man moving about in the shrubbery near the separate kitchen. He padded noiselessly towards the front of the house, passing dark windows. He was at the front of the house when he saw Bart Case standing there, looking almost directly at him, a cigar clenched between his teeth. The ripe odour of the rich tobacco was wafted to Chet. He raised the rifle.

Case did not move. For a long moment he stood there, looking directly at Chet, then he turned on a heel and walked into his room.

Chet wasted no time. He was over the rail, hanging on for a second, to drop lightly into the shrubbery. He bent low as he raced towards his horse. There was no one in sight. He ripped the reins loose, swung up into the saddle, hammered at the mount's flank with his rifle, then rode like the wind for the narrow foot-bridge spanning the *acequia*.

"What the hell!" yelled a man from the darkness.

A rifle crashed just as Chet reached the bridge. He hammered across it, hoping to God the horse would not slip, then he was into the field beyond, riding through the gathering light of the rising moon as rifles shattered the night and made the shadows bright with blossoms of fire. Slugs whined across the open fields as Chet's rangy mount slammed through the bosque at full tilt, cleared it, rode hard at a rail fence and rose to clear it and land lightly on the far side.

Chet King rode south as though the devil was squatting on his coat-tails, riding hard to get off Case land, and find a place to hide before the ant-heap he had disturbed was sufficiently organized to track him down. The fragrance of Theresa Case clung to his clothing, but there was no attraction in it for him. The odour to him now was akin to that of swollen bodies swelling beneath a summer sun in Tennessee or Mississippi during the war. The sickening cloying odour of human rot.

8

THE horse's hoofs rattled sharply on the gravelly bed of a shallow rivulet. Chet King turned in the saddle to look back across the rangeland. There was no sign of anyone in pursuit, but he couldn't delude himself on that point. Bart Case would be carrying the torch through the Highlands to rouse his clan of mercenaries and the orders would be to shoot to kill.

For the first time in years he was running by himself, and the loneliness struck him like a pole-axe. With Bung Burkbennett and the Kid to side him his chances would be fair enough. As it was, he was the lone target for Case's paid killers. In war a man can be captured and live, and even the Mexicans he had fought against after the war sometimes kept a man prisoner instead of giving him the *ley del fuego*, giving him a chance to run, *if* he can outrun hot lead looking for him as a target.

He turned quickly again as he heard the muffled thudding of hoofs on the road to his right. A man was riding hard, slashing at the rump of his horse with a stick. Chet kneed his horse into a bosque and dropped to the ground, ripping his Winchester from its scabbard as he did so. The horse trotted into the deeper shadows out of sight. The moon struck the face of the man as he turned to look back. It was Vicente Casias, the man who had supposedly witnessed the gun fight in the street between Chet and the man he had killed. Benny Tibbetts. Naked fear was etched on the face of Vicente Casias.

It was then that Chet heard an echo of the drumming of Vicente's horse on the road, but in an instant he knew that it wasn't an echo. There were other horsemen on that shadowy road, riding hard behind Vicente Casias. For a moment Chet almost called out to the man, but then he saw the two men who were pursuing Vicente. One of them was the youngest of the Tibbetts brothers, the vacant faced one named Harv, but this night his face was not vacant. It was etched with the hunting look; the look of a killer.

Chet raised his rifle and as quickly lowered it. He had his bellyful of trouble for that night, and the nights to come. Maybe Vicente Casias could outrun them. Maybe . . . After all, re- flected Chet, he *is* a Case man. Let Bart Case take care of his own.

Harv and his companion vanished down the road after the fleeing Vicente like foxhunters following the hounds to get the brush. Chet dared a smoke. He sat with his back against a tree and his rifle across his thighs. The impulse was strong within him to run and keep on running, but there was one thing he had to do first. He walked to the horse and led it through the bosque and along a dry ditch, thence out on a road that seemed as though it had not been used very much in recent times.

The moon had not yet flooded down into the area where the Miles ranch was situated. Chet took his time in approaching the place. He remembered all too well that Nancy Miles seemed right handy with the long gun.

The place was quiet. A single window was lighted by lamplight. Chet left the horse in a draw and walked towards the house, testing the cool night air with eyes, nose and ears. The sense that he depended on most, that honed sixth sense that had saved his life so many times he could hardly remember the number of them, seemed quiet that night.

He worked his way past the barn and stopped near the rear of the house. The light came from the small kitchen and even as he watched her shapely form passed between the window and the lamp on the table. He whistled softly. Minutes ticked past. He whistled again. The light flicked out. His keen hearing let him know that the rear door of the house had been opened, and the shadows on the back porch thickened.

"Nancy?" he called out.

"Is that you, Chet?" she answered.

"Yes." He walked slowly forward. "Are you alone?"

"Only my father is here. He's asleep."

He stopped at the edge of the porch and looked in amusement at the rifle in her slim hands. "Seems every time I come calling you meet me with that Spencer," he said.

She laughed, then placed the rifle on a bench. "I'm sorry," she said. "What is it you want?"

He felt inside his shirt pocket and took out the receipt Bart Case had written out and signed under Chet's gun muzzle. "This is a receipt, signed by Bart Case, for a thousand dollars," he said. "It clears your note."

Even in the dimness he could see the startled

look on her face. "I can't believe that," she said quietly.

"Read it," he said simply.

She lighted a match and read it. "It's his handwriting and signature all right," she said. "Who paid it, Chet?"

He leaned his rifle against a post and felt for the makings.

"Chet?" she said.

He looked at her. "I did," he said.

"Then we owe you instead of him?"

He waved a hand. "You can pay me when you get around to it."

She studied him. The moon was beginning to throw faint light into the valley. "I wish I could figure you out," she said. "Where's your star?"

He smiled. "We had a little disagreement. I suppose you could say I traded him the star for that receipt."

"Do you know what this means?"

He shrugged. "I was getting tired of working for Bart Case anyway."

She came closer to him. "You don't know the man! You don't know that family!"

"What do you mean by that?"

"Come inside if you mean to smoke that cigarette." She glanced up at the hills surrounding the house. "A good rifleman can use that lighted cigarette for a target."

He followed her into the house, picking up the rifles as he did so. He lighted the cigarette. "Put out the lamp," he said. "We can talk in the living-room, *without* light."

She did as she was told. They sat together on the horsehair settee in the dark living-room. "You said something the last time we talked," he said. "This time your heart won't let you allow Dad to get off the hook, you said. I asked if you meant Bart Case, and you said that it was *one* of the Cases. Who did you mean?"

"Don't you know, Chet?"

"Theresa?"

"Exactly."

Chet nodded. Theresa's proposition came back to him. She had been willing to trade her body to hold the man she had selected to succeed her father. She was hard and unyielding as he was, and Chet had a mind that she would be as ruthless as he was once she took the reins of power in her hands. Maybe more so.

"She's afraid," said Nancy simply.

He laughed shortly. "Not so you could notice it."

She eyed him in the darkness. "She wanted you, didn't she, Chet?"

He nodded. "I don't feel flattered about it," he said. "She didn't want Chet King, the lover, she wanted Chet King the fighting Texican. It's as simple as that." He leaned back against the wall behind the settee. "What is she so afraid about, conceding the point that you just might be right."

"If she had been born a man, she wouldn't be afraid, Chet. Hard as she is, she still can't handle her father's organization as well as a man could. A man like you, Chet."

"The major seems to be doing pretty well," said Chet drily.

"For how long?" she said.

He looked quickly at her. "He seems to be in good enough health."

"It isn't that, Chet. Haven't you noticed anything about him? Something different? Something that he is still concealing from the world?"

He stared at her. Memories came back to him. Something that had been hovering in the back of his mind ever since the first time he had talked to Case.

"Time is running short for Bart Case. One

day the people who fear him will find out something about him that his power and money cannot hide from them. I found out the last time I saw him. When I went in to see him about our note. He refused to see me, to talk to me at any rate, but I could see him in his office. When we had to sell our cattle, no one dared bid against his price. He came out himself to select the best of the herd at the lowest of prices. It was then I noticed that it was Theresa Case and Jose Silva who actually picked out the cattle."

Chet slowly took the cigarette from his mouth. He well remembered meeting Case on the balcony of his big house that very evening. The man had looked directly at him, then had walked casually back into his room. Facing a man who would have killed him had he made a move. A man who had the drop on him. He remembered other things too. How the major had sat in his unlighted office the first time Chet had met him. How he had felt about for his hat that hung on the wall. How he had bumped into his desk as he had walked towards Chet. How he had walked directly into the path of Benny Tibbetts the night the man had tried to ride him down and kill him. *He hadn't been able to see Tibbetts!*

"The sabre scar across his left temple," said Chet slowly. He looked at Nancy. "No wonder he made the mistake of giving me over twelve hundred dollars the night I saved his life in Two Rivers. At the time I didn't realize he might have made a mistake. I pocketed the lion's share of it, then split the rest with my companeros. Not that I was cheating them," he added quickly, "but those two loco Texicans would have been drunk for a week if I had split twelve hundred dollars with them. Case told me I would keep the account straight. No wonder he didn't count out the money! He couldn't!"

"I can imagine what that had done to his rapacity," she said. *"He can't even count his illgotten gains."*

She stood up and paced back and forth. "Theresa knows, Chet. She has been frightened that others would find out before she could find a man to help her hold Major Case's power." She laughed softly. "There was a time when she thought it might have been Jose Silva."

He narrowed his eyes. "Silva?"

"He was the big thing with her for a long time," she said. "Before him it was Charley

Tibbetts. But Charley was a little too head-strong to suit Theresa. They say she went to Texas to find a cousin of hers who had quite a reputation as a gunfighter. She came back without him."

"But found *me*," said Chet drily.

"Vicente Casias told me in town that Jose knew she was pushing him out in favour of you, Chet."

Chet remembered something else. How cold Silva had been with him. He remembered too the rifle shot from the bosque that could easily have killed him that moonlit night. There had been many cigarette butts pushed into the soft earth as the bushwhacker had waited for a shot at Chet. Jose Silva was hardly ever without a cigarette dangling from the corner of his thin mouth. Things had been moving too quickly for Chet to make an inventory of them; they were beginning to make sense now.

She came closer to him and placed a cool, slim hand against his face. "And you paid off our debt with the very money Major Case had given you?"

He grinned. "Seems like the biter got bit in that instance, Nancy."

She bent her head and touched his lips with

hers. "For paying the debt I thank you, Chet, but I don't think it will save the ranch for us. Bart Close will never let you get away with making a fool of him."

He shrugged. "What can he do?"

Her eyes held his. "You don't know him, even yet, or her either, Chet. You don't know them! The lengths to what they will go."

"Legally you're safe."

"Legally," she echoed quietly. "Now you had better get out of here. Run for your life, Chet!"

He stood up and drew her close. "Run? I've been running too long, Nancy. Ever since the war it seems I have been running. A man has to make a stand some time or another in his life. Maybe it will change the balance. Maybe it will show me the way."

She searched his face. "You mean you intend to stay here in the valley?"

"You can't move your father, and I'm not foolish enough to think Bart Case, *and* his lovely daughter, will let you stay on this land, whether the debt was paid or not."

"I have to stay," she said. "I can't leave him, but there's nothing here to hold you, Chet. You might find your death here, fighting in a hope-less cause."

"I've fought in a few hopeless causes in my time," he said quietly. "The best thing for us to do is get out of here, for a time at least. Can he travel at all?"

She shook her head. "It might kill him."

"It might kill him if he stays here."

Once again in Chet King's life of war and violence he found himself on the piercing horns of a dilemma. He had never run during the war. That had come in later years, when his heart was really never in any cause for which he fought. He had been a true mercenary. It wasn't himself he was concerned about, nor even Frank Miles, for the man was very ill, perhaps even now the seeds of death were within him. Chet had seen too many men with that look on their faces. The look as though the bony foundation of the head, beneath the taut skin, was trying to force its way through, a little before it was due. As though the skull meant to have its freedom from mortal flesh.

He raised his head. He walked quickly to the front door. The area was bathed in moonlight. His hearing had picked up the stumbling steps of a man, and somehow he knew those footsteps

140

heralded a man half frightened to death. "Stay back!" he said to Nancy.

He eased the door open a little further. A man had come from the shadows and was running awkwardly towards the house, as though one of his legs had been injured. His left arm swung easily and rhythmically back and forth as though it had been shattered. He looked back over his shoulder and then tried to spur himself onward. He looked with wide and desperate eyes towards the silent house. It was the fear haunted face of Vicente Casias.

Hoofs thudded on the road where the tree shadows were thick. A man laughed. "Keep arunnin', Casias!" he shouted. "How far you think you're going to get, hombre? Haw! Haw!" It was the loose voice of Harv Tibbetts.

Chet knew then what was wrong with Casias. They had evidently been playing with the man. Probably had shot his horse out from under him, injuring his leg and breaking his arm. They had winged their bird and were now moving in for the kill.

Casias reached out a hand towards the house, then fell heavily. As he raised his head the moonlight showed the red stained white of his left sleeve. He looked back over his shoulder and saw his two pursuers dismounting. Then he pressed his face hard against the ground. His body trembled like the leaves of a quaking aspen.

Harv Tibbetts was grinning like a death's head in the moonlight. He walked slowly towards the fallen man. His belled spurs jingled musically in a slow rhythm of death. "Get up, Casias, you lying sonofabitch," he said. "Get up and take it like a man."

The other man came up behind Harv. "Watch out for Frank Miles," he said. "He won't like this, Harv."

Harv laughed. "You're too nervous, Larry," he said. "Ol' Frank can't get out'a his bed." He grinned. "I'd like to see Nance in *her* bed, unable to get out. Haw! I'd keep her company all right!"

Chet felt as though he had been lashed across the face with a whip of cholla. He dropped his hand to his Colt. He hoped to God that Nancy hadn't heard Harv.

Harv grinned. "Get up, hombre!" he said.

"For the love of God, Senor Tibbetts!" pleaded Vicente.

As swift as the hard sure thrust of a diamondback's flat and ugly head came the drawing of

Harv's nickle-plated Colt. It crashed, awakening the drowsy echoes in the sleepy hills. Vicente jumped spasmodically. His right arm was flung outward at an awkward angle and blood began to soak through the dingy white cloth of his sleeve.

"Haw!" roared Harv. "Get up, you bastard!"

Harv didn't see the lean shadow that seemed to detach itself from beneath the darkness of the ramada that shaded the front porch of the house. It was Larry who saw it. "For Christ's sake, Harv!" he yelled as he drew. "It's that damned Texican King!"

Chet crouched and fired, moving in swiftly. Larry spun about and fell heavily, his Colt exploding to send keening lead soaring into the moonlighted night. Harv jumped to one side and fired. The lead whispered past Chet's head. He fired just as Vicente rolled against Harv's feet, staggering the gunman.

Harv jumped to one side again, peering through the smoke, futiley fanning at it with his free hand. Then he saw death coming through the smoke. Death in the shape of a long-legged Texan. Harv fired, but an instant before he did so, the Texan's slug caught him just over the heart and he was dead before he hit the ground.

The echoes fled away to hide in the silver-lighted hills. The powdersmoke drifted lazily away from the yard. Chet King flicked open the loading gate of his smoking Colt and fed fresh cartridges into it. He holstered the weapon and knelt beside Vicente Casias.

Casias opened his eyes. "Gracias," he said. There was the faint glaze of death over his brown eyes. "It is not good to die like a slaughtered sheep."

"You may have saved my life, Vicente," said Chet.

"That dung in human form deserved to die."

"It was a brave thing to do. You are much of the man, Vicente."

"*Nada! Nada!* Nothing! Nothing." Vicente stiffened. "*Esta bien*. It is good. It is good that a man can give his life for another." Vicente raised his head. "Get out of this valley, amigo. They will hunt you down. You have killed two of them. You will now have to kill the other two, or *they* will kill you."

"I stay, amigo," said Chet.

"You are loco, but very brave. *Muy bravo!*"

144

Then Vicente stiffened. His head lolled sideways and he was gone.

She came from the house and looked down upon Chet. "He was right," she said.

"I'll stay, Nancy."

"Go while you have time, Chet!"

He raised his head. "Listen," he said. "It is too late."

The muffled thudding of many hoofs came to them on the night wind. The hoofs of horses ridden by hostile men.

Chet worked quickly, manhandling the three bodies into the barn. He buried them in hay and straw, then pulled a buckboard in front of the hiding place. He ran outside and slapped the two horses on the rumps. They trotted towards a bosque.

Chet ran towards the house. There were three dark patches on the ground. The death blood of three men. They could hardly be missed. There could be no running now. The sands of fate were trickling swiftly. The Fates were grinning down on Chet King. Two of them had finished their work. One had spun the thread of his life, the second had measured it, the third squatted with poised shears to cut the thread.

He closed the door behind him and placed

the bar across it. It was a good house. It had been built like a small fortress during the days when the Jicarillas ravaged that country, and bandidos were as common as salt.

Nancy had shuttered the windows. They were well made, with thick wood sandwiching sheet metal between them, and the doors were fashioned the same way. She leaned her Spencer against the wall and looked at him. "It's too late now," she said.

"I'm sorry for you."

She smiled. "No, Chet. At least we are together."

He drew her close and kissed her. When he raised his head again there was no sound of hoofs against the road.

9

THE wind blew softly down the valley and whispered about the ranch buildings. The shadows danced about beneath the trees. The area was bathed in clear, silvery moonlight, and the edges of the still shadows were as sharp as though drawn with a ruling pen against the whitish ground. There was no sign of life amongst the trees and brush, or the darkened buildings. To a man like Chet King, whose life had been one of war and violence for the past twelve years or so, the very quietness was mute warning, and the shifting shadows seemed alive with malignancy. They were out there all right. He didn't know who *they* were as yet, but there was nothing friendly about them. He could sense that like the smell from a long used privy.

A tall, broad-shouldered man moved quickly from one shadow to another. "You in there, Frank Miles?" he called out. It was the harsh voice of Charley Tibbetts.

Chet looked at Nancy. "Answer him," he said.

She opened a shutter. "What do you want, Charley?"

"I want to talk to your old man."

"He's very ill. I don't want him disturbed."

Tibbetts laughed. "He'll be a hulluva lot more disturbed if we come in there," he said.

"What is it you want?"

"My brother," said Tibbetts. "We found a dead horse in the hills. Belonged to Vicente Casias. My brother came this way with Larry Mulvihill. Where are they?"

"I haven't seen them."

"She's lying, Charley," said Irv Tibbetts from the shadows. "Let's cut out the fooling around. We found the horses in the bosque, didn't we? Harv and Larry must be in there."

"Open up your house," said Charley. "We won't bother you or your old man."

She laughed. "That'll be quite a change for you."

"Listen you! If Harv is in there we're coming in to get him."

Nancy looked at Chet. He shrugged. "Keep talking. Maybe you can convince him."

"Why would he be in here?" said Nancy.

Irv laughed. "At any other time we'd have a good idea. He always did have his eye on you, Nance."

Charley moved again. He was looking directly at the house. Chet hefted his rifle. He could drive a slug into the big man through a loophole and Tibbetts would never know what had hit him. There were too many of the others out there. At least a dozen of them.

"Hey, Charlie!" called out another man. "We found another hoss in a draw. Looks like the hoss that bigmouthed Texan was riding."

"*Which* bigmouthed Texan?" asked Charley. "They *all* got big mouths."

"Haw!" cried Irv in delight.

"The one named King," said the man.

The following silence seemed to hang like powdersmoke over the ranch. Charley vanished into the darkness.

"You're disturbing my father!" called out Nancy.

"Is Chet King in there?" asked Charley.

"No."

"You're lying! Look, you tell him to come out'a there, with his hands up, or his sixgun working, or, by God, we'll come in and get him!"

Chet leaned against the wall and rolled a cigarette. "They know I'm in here," he said, almost as though to himself.

"What can we do?"

Chet shrugged. He lighted the cigarette and blew out a ring of smoke. He idly watched the smoke lift and waver, then drift towards a crack in one of the shutters. "Fight," he said drily. "I can always do as they say."

"No," she said.

He picked up his rifle. "It's better that way."

"No, Chet!"

He reached for the door bar. Maybe he'd fight his way through; maybe they'd let the girl and her father alone if he went out there to face them.

She moved quickly, snatching up her Spencer repeater. She thrust it through a shutter loophole, and before he could stop her she had fired. The report thundered in the closed room. Smoke swirled back about Nancy. She turned and looked at him with a set look on her lovely face. "Now we'll fight it out together!" she said.

Her shot triggered a dozen others. Lead whined past the house or slapped into the thick adobe. Several slugs thudded into the thick shutters.

"Nancy!" called out Frank Miles.

She ran to his room. Chet could hear them talking in low voices. He took his cigarette from his lips and flipped it into the beehive fireplace. There would be no way out of this mess now. Salt, pepper, and gravel in the grease. The Tibbetts corrida were as thick out there as fiddlers in hell.

He padded from one window to the other until he caught sight of a booted foot thrust out from beneath a bush. He aimed at it and fired. The big slug ripped off the boot heel and the wearer of the boot shot bolt upright from the stinging impact against his foot in time to get a second slug slammed into his right shoulder. He went down clawing for a mane hold on the harsh ground, screaming his guts out.

Chet padded to the rear of the house listening to the devilish woodpecker din of hot lead against the moonlighted walls. A searching slug found a loophole and whistled through, hot for blood, to smash a Rogers group that sat on the marble-topped table in the centre of the room.

Chet paused at a window. It was just about the time for the boys to get their wide loop completely around the house, and they'd likely stay up high. Sure enough he saw a man dart

151

from one boulder to another, and vanish from sight, only to poke his head up beyond the boulder, just in time to get a softnosed slug through the top of his head. He rolled over and down the slope, arms and legs flying, jerking like a marionette on a string, to end up like a bundle of rags against a tree, with the bright moonlight on his blood masked face.

"You fight like a professional," she said behind him.

"I am," he said drily. "Come to think of it, Nancy, it's my trade, my stock in goods, my only education."

"You can go on to other things," she said.

He turned and looked at her. "*Now?*" he said.

"You don't think we'll get out of this?"

He walked to a side window and peered through a shutter in time to see a man running for cover. He helped him along with a whistling slug. In answer a slug slapped into the adobe and cast shards of it through the loophole. One of them flicked across his cheek. He raised a hand and wiped away the thin trickle. "There's your answer," he said.

It grew quiet again except for the incessant whispering of the dry wind. Chet reloaded his rifle. He gathered every gun he could find and loaded them, shotguns, rifles, and pistols, placing them in the various rooms, ready for instant use. If they rushed the place they'd need every weapon they could get.

"King!" called out Charley Tibbetts. "Where's my brother?"

Chet did not answer. He lighted a cigarette.

"Harv?" called out Irv Tibbetts. "You in there? Larry?"

No answer but from the whispering wind.

They would have their ring about the house now. No chance to make a break. Rifle fire could kill a dozen men before they could reach cover across that moonlit ground, and by the same token, no man could reach the house across it. Not until the moon crossed the western hills and died away. When the darkness closed in, the Tibbetts corrida would close in, peddling death from barking guns.

Chet raised his head. More horses. How many men followed Charley Tibbetts? How many more slit-eyed marksmen were riding through the night to weave the meshes of the net ever tighter about that darkened house?

A shot blasted the quiet. "It's Major Case,

Charley!" yelled a man from the darkness along the road.

The silence flowed through the valley again. Then Chet heard the low murmuring of voices from the road. He could vaguely see many men amongst the trees. Major Case had come in strength. Chet rolled a cigarette, wondering if Bungo and the Kid were with the Case corrida. He lighted the cigarette. It didn't really matter.

Twenty minutes had ticked past, and still no shooting from the men on the road, just the steady murmuring of voices. Nancy came close beside Chet and he slipped an arm about her slender waist. He could feel the steady beating of her heart.

"King?" called out Charley Tibbetts.

"You know I'm in here!" called out Chet.

"Major Case is here with his men. We've agreed for a truce between us."

"To get me, eh?" called Chet.

"You've got the idea. Now, once more, come out with your hands up. We won't bother the girl and her father."

"With Bart Case out there? That rapacious wolf wouldn't let Jesus alone in peace on the shores of the Sea of Galilee!"

"Very witty, King," said a cold voice from

the shadows. "Now give us the *right* answer."
It was Bart Case.

The wolves had gathered to kill off another
wolf. A lone wolf who had decided not to run
with the pack. Tibbetts and Case were strange
bedfellows indeed. They must want Chet King's
heart blood badly enough to forget their own
differences, for a time at least.

Chet raised his rifle. Maybe he could get
Charley Tibbetts, or the major, and by a stroke
of miraculous luck, the both of them. That
might break up the alliance, and the siege. He
sighted at a man standing near an outbuilding,
silhouetted against the light wood of the struc-
ture. The man moved. Chet lowered the rifle.
It was Theresa Case.

"You might have been better off to kill her,"
said Nancy quietly. "She'll never rest now until
you're dead, Chet."

Nancy was right. It wasn't in Chet King to
kill a woman. Not yet anyway. Time might
make a difference.

The men on the road faded into the shifting
shadows. Case's men would fill in the gaps in
the ring that surrounded the house. Not even a
rabbit could break for cover from that house
now.

It was quiet again. A brooding quiet that seemed to flow about the house like some aura of evil. They would wait until darkness. That would be the limit of time. Darkness . . .

Nancy went into the kitchen to make coffee. The strong odour of the brew drifted throughout the house. Frank Miles called to Chet from the bedroom. His face was gaunt and wet with sweat. "Maybe you should have forgotten about us, King," he said. "This will lead to nothing but slaughter. I wish I had sent Nancy away."

"She wouldn't have left," said Chet.

Miles nodded. "You're right. Can't we make a deal with them?"

"*You* might."

The rancher eyed Chet. "They mean to kill you?"

"I haven't any doubt about it. I broke the law of the pack. It made an unholy alliance between Tibbetts and Case. They seem to have forgotten their differences in favour of getting me, Miles."

The rancher waved a hand. "I still think they can be reasoned with."

Chet shook his head. "I killed Benny Tibbetts and later Harv Tibbetts and a man named Larry Mulvihill. I owe the remaining two Tibbetts a blood debt. I bearded Bart Case in his own den. That was a death sentence for me, Miles."

The rancher closed his eyes. "It's hard for a man to die this way."

"You'll live, Miles."

The rancher shook his head. "I haven't long, King."

There was no use in arguing with him. As a matter of fact, none of them might have long to live. Chet knew he was facing the last fight of his life. Trapped in a house with a girl and a dying man. Even Bungo and the Kid could hardly swing the balance in his favour. They were well out of this thing. The thought came to him that the two of them might be out there in the cold shadows, watching the house with slitted eyes, waiting for Chet to make his break. He couldn't blame them. They were mercenaries as he was. They fought for pay, and the highest bidder would gain their skilled services. It was as simple as that.

Chet walked into the living-room and to a side window. He unlatched a shutter and eased it open. He hit the floor an instant before a bullet smashed into the shutter.

"Chet?" she called from the kitchen.

He closed the shutter and went to her. "I was just experimenting," he said. "Damned fool thing to do."

After he had his coffee he made the rounds of the house, studying each of the outbuildings, each boulder, each shadow on the hillside, until he had a fair idea of how many of them there were out there. Some of them were in the outbuildings. Some of them were in the barn, still ignorant of the fact that three dead men lay beneath the straw and hay. When Charley and Irv Tibbetts found their brother, the second of them to be killed by Chet King they'd go to the very gates of hell to get the man who had killed them.

The moon was already slanting down over the hills, moving faster to Chet's peace of mind than he would have liked. He had racked his brain to figure out a way to save Nancy and her father, and there just wasn't any answer. Those men out there were safe enough in their killings, for the thin guise of being sheriff had always stood Bart Case in good stead. It gave the Case corrida carte blanche to commit legal murder.

Now and then, at almost regular intervals, a

bullet would pock the thick adobe, or smack into a shutter. Sometimes they would keen eerily off into space. It seemed almost impersonal to Chet King. A man who knows he is doomed, can sometimes detach himself from worldly matters, but not for long.

She sat on the settee, with her back against the wall, a vagrant ray of moonlight dimly lighting her lovely face. Now and then he would look at her, but they did not speak. Conversation was hardly important now. But to find someone for whom you had been looking all your life only to lose her shortly after you had found her was hard indeed.

The darkness was coming with the swiftness of sudden death. There was nothing to do now but wait for the quick, killing rush from the shadows. The rifles and pistols were loaded, and the shotguns were ready, loaded with buck and ball for the last desperate stand.

Then suddenly the moonlight was gone and the valley was shrouded in the darkness. The night seemed to be breathing like some primordial monster, wetting its thick loose lips, sure of its helpless prey.

Chet stood by the door, rifle in hand, fully cocked, between the coming attackers and the girl, rather a foolish gesture, but gallant. The passing gallantry of a man who had thought for many years that he had left his heart in the dead ashes of the Confederacy.

Time flicked past, then seemed to slow down in the final waiting minutes.

The area was thick in darkness.

Chet wetted his dry lips. He tried to cut a view through the darkness with his eyes but it was no use.

The flickering of flame came to him at the very moment he caught the resinous scent of burning wood. He ran to a loophole and peered through it to see one of the outbuildings alight, casting the rising glow on the bare ground.

"What is it, Chet?" she called.

He turned. "They've fired a shed to give them light." He grinned reassuringly. "The fools! The darkness was best for them." He looked quickly away before she could really read his face. If they would fire the shed, they'd fire the barn, and if they fired the barn they'd know soon enough that dead men had been concealed within the barn. That would trigger the assault on the house, *if they didn't fire the house first to drive Chet into the open* . . .

Now and then he'd fire a shot into the

160

shadows, probing for a target, but all he got in return was the whiplash cracking of a rifle echoing his, and a slug rapping almost into the very loophole he fired from.

There would be no attrition from his firing. He'd never wear them down.

The shed flared up high and crackled intensely for a time, then it collapsed, sending up a swirling shower of sparks. Some of them drifted over to a small building near the barn. For a time nothing happened, and then a spot of red, like a ruby on velvet, began to grow on the roof of the building, and by the time the first outbuilding was nothing but a thick mass of embers, the second building was blazing merrily.

The wind shifted and the smoke drifted towards the house and began to seep through cracks and the loopholes. Frank Miles began to cough, and it never stopped, a dry hacking thing that got on Chet's nerves. Even the bullets didn't seem to bother him as much as the coughing.

The wind shifted again and the flames leaped higher, high enough for Chet to see a man dart hastily for cover. He never made it. A slug broke his spine and he lay there in the gathering pool of light with his clothing starting to smoulder from fat sparks.

The barn was next. It was getting close to midnight now. The flames started from low down, in a corner, and licked greedily up the side of the dry, warped siding until it reached the eaves, then it quested along beneath the eaves until it clawed a foothold on the shingles. A runnel of flame flicked towards the ridge of the roof and danced erratically until it got hold, then it settled down to the real business at hand. Holes appeared in the roof. Pieces of burning wood thudded down inside the burning building, sending up showers of fat sparks, spreading the good work.

In forty-five minutes a new odour began to mingle with that of burning wood and hay. The odour of burning flesh. Human flesh.

Chet could hear excited voices behind the blazing building. A rear door crashed open. Gas and flame leaped high. Boots thudded on the hard ground. Then Charley Tibbetts yelled into the flaming night. He yelled like a man gone suddenly loco, and Chet King knew that they had found the bullet holed body of Harv Tibbetts.

After that the fusillade started. Soft slugs

smashed into the walls, shutters, and doors. The wind began to fishtail, sweeping smoke and sparks from the barn towards the besieged house and then away again. It mingled with the powdersmoke and cast a thick pall over the ranch until the place looked like a close-in suburb of hell itself.

The barn collapsed, sending up a thick, swirling column of smoke and sparks that drifted down the valley, scattering fire into the river. It grew uncomfortably hot in the house. Sweat dripped from Chet's face as he returned the fire. Heat, if nothing else, might drive them from the house. It grew hotter and suddenly, like the knell of coming doom, a great patch of plaster fell from the ceiling to crash onto the table. Chet stopped firing. He turned and looked at the ceiling. The roof was ablaze. They were trapped in a man-made oven big enough to roast three people, if they didn't make a break into the firelit open and sudden death from dozens of slugs.

Patch after patch of plaster fell. Then a hole appeared in the ceiling of the living-room. A hole edged with snapping, crackling flames. A beam cracked and the roof began to sag a little.

Chet reloaded his rifle. He checked his Colt

and took a spare, thrusting it beneath his belt. He placed several rifles near the front door.

Glass shattered in the gathering heat. Plaster thudded to the floor in Nancy's bedroom. Smoke flowed into the living-room from the kitchen.

"See to your father," he cried.

"What can I do?" she cried.

"We can't stay here."

She ran to the bedroom and vanished in the smoke. He could hear her coughing and calling out to her father. Then she was back in the living-room, with a strange look on her face. "He's gone," she said.

Chet ran into the room. The bed was empty. He whirled and saw that a window gaped open. He darted to it in time to see the tall, gaunt figure of Frank Miles, a double-barrelled shotgun tucked beneath his right armpit and his hand gripping the small of the stock, trigger finger pressing the first of the two triggers. It was the thick smoke that gave him his chance to get from the house.

"Bart Case!" yelled Frank Miles. "Come out into the open and let's finish this thing man to man!"

"Oh my God!" said Nancy from behind

Chet. She tried to get to the window but he forced her back.

"This is our only chance, Nancy," he said. "He's sacrificing himself for us."

Then the haunting rebel yell seemed to rip through the smoke and flames, and Frank Miles, once a fighting man with Terry's Texas Rangers, went into his last fight.

10

THE seeming apparition of the gaunt Texan, with the stamp of death on his face, coming through the smoke towards his enemies held them motionless long enough for Miles to reach close-in range for the big double gun. A man stepped out from behind a tree and raised his rifle. One barrel of the shotgun blasted flame and smoke and the man went down, dying as he fell.

"Bart Case!" yelled Miles. He gave vent to the piercing and thrilling rebel yell. A bullet thudded into his flesh spinning him halfway round. Another bullet drove him backward. A third bullet glanced from the shot gun. One of Case's men, the one named Adolfo, jumped out into the flickering firelight. "I will kill him, *patron*!" he cried back over his shoulder. He never made good his promise, for the second barrel of the shotgun spat flame and smoke and the heavy charge tore into Adolfo's chest. Miles screeched the rebel yell as he hurled the empty shotgun at his enemies and drew a Colt from his waistband.

"Come on!" yelled Chet at Nancy. He gripped her by the arm and dragged her towards the kitchen just as her father opened fire with his sixgun. Many of the Tibbetts and Case men were running towards the shooting.

Chet ripped free the bar that was across the kitchen door and jerked the door open. Smoke hung in rifted veils across the rear of the burning house. Great sparks floated serenely through the hot air, alighting here and there, starting fresh fires.

A man rounded the corner and met a softnosed slug head-on. His partner reeled sideways when Chet's second shot broke his shoulder. "They're breaking out the back, Major Case!" he yelled as he fell to the ground.

Chet shoved Nancy ahead of him, trying to cover her from the flying bullets, and knowing all the time only a miracle would get them safe into the dark hills.

Four men rounded the other side of the house. Guns were still barking at the front of the house as Frank Miles fought his last fight, this time to the death. The quartet ran towards

Chet and Nancy. He shoved her towards a tree and whirled to face them.

"Look out!" screamed Nancy. "There are two of them behind you, Chet!"

Chet glanced over his shoulder to see them. His eyes slitted. There was no mistaking Bungo Burkbennett and the Kid. "Stay back!" he yelled. "Stay back, or by God, I'll kill the both of you!"

"Get out'a the way, Chet," said the Kid.

Chet raised his rifle. "Stand back!"

Bungo spat to one side. "Get out'a the way, Cap'n King, and we'll show you how real Texicans handle these yahoos!" He fired from the hip. The first of the quartet went down. The Kid fired his twin Colts. The second man went down. Bungo got the third of the four of them.

The Kid grinned at Chet through the smoke. "You goin' to just stand there, Chet?"

Chet's rifle blasted from his hip and the fourth man joined the others. "Come on," he said. "I think we've got work to do up front, companeros!"

Three men rounded the front of the house, walking into the wreathing smoke towards the sprawled body of Frank Miles, dead with six slugs in his body and with his empty sixgun clenched in his stiffening hand.

It was Jose Silva who gave the alarm as he saw the three Texans. His white teeth flashed in the firelight. "This time there is no escape, Texican!" he spat at Chet. His rifle flashed. The slug plucked at Chet's left sleeve, triggering his reaction. A bullet caught Jose Silva in the mouth, smashing his lovely set of teeth, but then he'd never use them again anyway.

Bungo Burkbennett fired and dropped a man, then reeled back through the smoke as a slug drove through his right forearm. He did the border shift and dropped another man.

The Kid was inspired. He seemed to wade through the mingled smoke from the fire and the thickening powdersmoke, sixguns flashing alternately as he placed each shot.

Chet's rifle ran dry and he hurled it into the contorted face of Irv Tibbetts, drawing and firing his Colt from the hip to send Irv down with a slug through the right thigh, shattering the bone. A bullet whipped past Chet's left cheek, drawing blood, and in the quick pain of the wound he reeled sideways against a tree. It was then that Charley Tibbetts saw his chance. He fired and the slug pocked the tree an inch behind Chet's head. His second shot tore through Chet's hat. His third shot keened into space as Chet dropped to the ground and fired upward, the slug catching Charley in the guts.

The Tibbetts and Case men broke for the woods, trying to get away from the three cold-eyed Texans and the slugs that tore after them as they ran.

The roof of the burning house collapsed, sending up a great gush of gas and flame. A wave of hot air engulfed the Texans. Through it, Chet saw Theresa Case giving her father a hand up into the saddle. She ran along beside his horse, leading the mare. Chet plunged after them, though he didn't really know why. At the far edge of the bosque she turned and raised a nickel-plated pistol, the same one she had used the day she and her cousin had been trapped in the stagecoach at Hueco Tanks. "It's Chet King, Father!" she cried.

Bart Case wrenched savagely at the reins of his horse. The bay reared and plunged, driving Theresa against a tree. She seemed to rebound back towards the horse and as she did so the forehoofs struck against her, sending her down to the ground. Case fired at Chet. The slug whistled past his head. The touchy horse reared and slammed off at full gallop through the dark woods. Case turned and fired blindly behind him again and again, but Chet just stood there watching the man as he raced through the woods. Then Chet heard a hard thudding sound and the horse went on, plunging through the river shallows, but he had left the major behind.

Chet ran towards the man. The major hung from a limb crotch, his legs thrashing spasmodically, and then he hung limply. His pistol dropped to the ground.

Chet looked up into the contorted face of the man he had hated. Case's neck had been snapped as neatly as though he had fallen through the trap of the gallows. Chet gripped the man's legs, lifted him, and then lowered him to the ground. Case's eyes were wide open, but they did not see. Death had blinded him before his old war wound had finished the job while the man was still alive.

Chet walked back to Theresa. She lay quite still. The shooting was over. Smoke drifted through the trees. The crackling of the flames that still ate away at the house came to them. She looked at him with those great gold flecked eyes of hers. "Where is my father?" she asked.

He looked back through the woods but did not speak.

"Did he escape?" she asked. She laughed a little, then winced in savage pain. "My father. Barton Case. *Major* Barton Case. I asked you if he escaped." She laughed again and a thin trickling of blood came from the corner of her mouth. "Escaped from you, Chet King. A man like *him*. A *real* man! Running away from the likes of rebel scum like you."

"Don't talk," he said softly. He knelt beside her but she feebly pushed him back. She closed her eyes. The white blouse beneath her riding coat was rapidly darkening with blood.

The wind shifted and drove the smoke up the valley. Chet brushed her hair back from her lovely face, and the look of coming death upon it was plain to see. She opened her eyes. "We could have made it, Texan," she said. "You and I together. We could have handled this valley, eh, Texan?"

He nodded.

"You had the skill and the guts," she said. She coughed again. "I had the brains. But you're soft inside, Texan. We would have tried to kill each other one way or another, by thought or deed."

172

The flow of blood was thicker now. She coughed spasmodically. "You won. I don't know how you did it. You, and Bungo and the Kid." She laughed a little. "You saved my life at Hueco Tanks to take it here. Now that snivelling cousin of mine will inherit everything. *Everything* do you hear?"

Chet passed a hand across his dirty, powder-blackened face. A man can see only so much violence and death. It is not good for a man to see too much of death.

Her hand closed tightly on his. "God, Texan," she breathed thickly. "We could have bred a litter that would have run this valley, and maybe this territory for generations. Goodbye, Texan!"

She was gone. He touched her lips with his, then walked slowly through the woods towards the fires. The woman he loved was waiting there for him, but he knew deep in his heart that he'd never forget Theresa. A fighting man can hardly forget a woman like that.

He could hear the cries of the wounded, and their stifled curses. Bungo Burkbennett was seated on the ground while the Kid tied the last knot in the bandage about his forearm. He grinned at Chet. "By God, Cap'n," he said. "That was one of the best fights we ever had."

"I hope it's the last," said Chet. He looked at the Kid. "Go over to the Case hacienda, Kid. Tell her she's all alone now."

"Both of them gone, Chet?" asked the Kid. "The woman too?"

Chet nodded and they saw the deep hurt in his grey eyes. "Sarah is sole owner now, Kid. She'll need a good man beside her."

"I didn't figure it that way," said the Kid quietly. "It's Sarah I wanted, not the estate."

"I know, Kid. Get going! *Andele!* She'll need you beside her this night."

The Kid swung up on a horse and rode through the wreathing smoke towards the road. Bungo shifted. He looked at Chet. "Looks like the Kid might need a good ramrodder for that spread, Chet. You reckon he'll give me the job?"

Chet smiled. "Why not? He'll never find a better man, but maybe you'll have to call him Mister Carson."

"That'll be the day," said Bungo drily. "Look behind you, Cap'n."

Chet turned. She was coming towards him through the drifting smoke, and as she did so he

174

miraculously seemed to forget the Lost Cause, sudden death, Theresa Case, and everything else, for now none of them seemed to matter in the light of the eyes of the woman who loved him, and whom he loved in turn. Chet King had come home at last . . .

THE END

FIGHTING RAMROD
by Charles N. Heckelmann

Most men would have cut their losses, but Frazer counted the bullets in his guns and said he'd soak the range in blood before he'd give up another inch of what was his.

LONE GUN
by Eric Allen

Smoke Blackbird had been away too long. The Lequires had seized the Blackbird farm, forcing the Indians and settlers off, and no one seemed willing to fight! He had to fight alone.

THE THIRD RIDER
by Barry Cord

Mel Rawlins wasn't going to let anything stand in his way. His father was murdered, his two brothers gone. Now Mel rode for vengeance.

RIDE A LONE TRAIL
by Gordon D. Shirreffs

The valley was about to explode into open range war. All it needed was the fuse and Ken Macklin was it.

ARIZONA DRIFTERS
by W. C. Tuttle

When drifting Dutton and Lonnie Steelman decide to become partners they find that they have a common enemy in the formidable Thurston brothers.

TOMBSTONE
by Matt Braun

Wells Fargo paid Luke Starbuck to outgun the silver-thieving stagecoach gang at Tombstone. Before long Luke can see the only thing bearing fruit in this eldorado will be the gallows tree.

HIGH BORDER RIDERS
by Lee Floren

Buckshot McKee and Tortilla Joe cut the trail of a border tough who was running Mexican beef into Texas. They stopped the smuggler in his tracks.

HARD MAN WITH A GUN
by Charles N. Heckelmann

After Bob Keegan lost the girl he loved and the ranch he had sweated blood to build, he had nothing left but his guts and his guns but he figured that was enough.

BRETT RANDALL, GAMBLER
by E. B. Mann

Larry Day had the choice of running away from the law or of assuming a dead man's place. No matter what he decided he was bound to end up dead.

THE GUNSHARP
by William R. Cox

The Eggerleys weren't very smart. They trained their sights on Will Carney and Arizona's biggest blood bath began.

THE DEPUTY OF SAN RIANO
by Lawrence A. Keating and
Al. P. Nelson

When a man fell dead from his horse, Ed Grant was spotted riding away from the scene. The deputy sheriff rode out after him and came up against everything from gunfire to dynamite.

SUNDANCE: IRON MEN
by Peter McCurtin

Sundance, assigned to save the railroad from a murder spree, soon came to realise that he'd have to fight fire with fire, bullets with bullets and death with death!

FARGO: MASSACRE RIVER
by John Benteen

Fargo spurred his horse to the edge of the road. The ambushers up ahead had now blocked the road. Fargo's convoy was a jumble, a perfect target for the insurgents' weapons!

SUNDANCE:
DEATH IN THE LAVA
by John Benteen

The land echoed with the thundering hoofs of Modoc ponies. In minutes they swooped down and captured the wagon train and its cargo of gold. But now the halfbreed they called Sundance was going after it, and he swore nothing would stand in his way.

GUNS OF FURY
by Ernest Haycox

Dane Starr, alias Dan Smith, wanted to close the door on his past and hang up his guns, but people wouldn't let him. Good men wanted him to settle their scores for them. Bad men thought they were faster and itched to prove it. Starr had to keep killing just to stay alive.

FARGO: PANAMA GOLD
by John Benteen

Cleve Buckner was recruiting an army of killers, gunmen and deserters from all over Central America. With foreign money behind him, Buckner was going to destroy the Panama Canal before it could be completed. Fargo's job was to stop Buckner—and to eliminate him once and for all!

FARGO: THE SHARPSHOOTERS
by John Benteen

The Canfield clan, thirty strong, were raising hell in Texas. One of them had shot a Texas Ranger, and the Rangers had to bring in the killer. Fargo was tough enough to hold his own against the whole clan.

SUNDANCE: OVERKILL
by John Benteen

Sundance's reputation as a fighting man had spread. There was no job too tough for the halfbreed to handle. So when a wealthy banker's daughter was kidnapped by the Cheyenne, he offered Sundance $10,000 to rescue the girl.

HELL RIDERS
by Steve Mensing

Wade Walker's kid brother, Duane, was locked up in the Silver City jail facing a rope at dawn. Wade was a ruthless outlaw, but he was smart, and he had vowed to have his brother out of jail before morning!

DESERT OF THE DAMNED
by Nelson Nye

The law was after him for the murder of a marshal—a murder he didn't commit. Breen was after him for revenge—and Breen wouldn't stop at anything . . . blackmail, a frameup . . . or murder.

DAY OF THE COMANCHEROS
by Steven C. Lawrence

Their very name struck terror into men's hearts—the Comancheros, a savage army of cutthroats who swept across Texas, leaving behind a bloodstained trail of robbery and murder.

SUNDANCE: SILENT ENEMY
by John Benteen

Both the Indians and the U.S. Cavalry were being victimized. A lone crazed Cheyenne was on a personal war path against both sides. They needed to pit one man against one crazed Indian. That man was Sundance.

LASSITER
by Jack Slade

Lassiter wasn't the kind of man to listen to reason. Cross him once and he'd hold a grudge for years to come—if he let you live that long. But he was no crueler than the men he had killed, and he had never killed a man who didn't need killing.

LAST STAGE TO GOMORRAH
by Barry Cord

Jeff Carter, tough ex-riverboat gambler, now had himself a horse ranch that kept him free from gunfights and card games. Until Sturvesant of Wells Fargo showed up. Jeff owed him a favour and Sturvesant wanted it paid up. All he had to do was to go to Gomorrah and recover a quarter of a million dollars stolen from a stagecoach!

McALLISTER ON THE COMANCHE CROSSING
by Matt Chisholm

The Comanche, deadly warriors and the finest horsemen in the world, reckon McAllister owes them a life—and the trail is soaked with the blood of the men who had tried to outrun them before.

QUICK-TRIGGER COUNTRY
by Clem Colt

Turkey Red hooked up with Curly Bill Graham's outlaw crew and soon made a name for himself. But wholesale murder was out of Turk's line, so when range war flared he bucked the whole border gang alone . . .

PISTOL LAW
by Paul Evan Lehman

Lance Jones came back to Mustang for just one thing—Revenge! Revenge on the people who had him thrown in jail; on the crooked marshal; on the human vulture who had already taken over the town. Now it was Lance's turn . . .

GUNSLINGER'S RANGE
by Jackson Cole

Three escaped convicts are out for revenge. They won't rest until they put a bullet through the head of the dirty snake who locked them behind bars.

RUSTLER'S TRAIL
by Lee Floren

Jim Carlin knew he would have to stand up and fight because he had staked his claim right in the middle of Big Ike Outland's best grass. Jim also had a score to settle with his renegade brother.

Larry and Stretch:
THE TRUTH ABOUT SNAKE RIDGE
by Marshall Grover

The troubleshooters came to San Cristobal to help the needy. For Larry and Stretch the turmoil began with a brawl, then an ambush, and then another attempt on their lives—all in one day.

WOLF DOG RANGE
by Lee Floren

Montana was big country, but not big enough for a ruthless land-grabber like Will Ardery. He would stop at nothing, unless something stopped him first—like a bullet from Pete Manly's gun.

Larry and Stretch: DEVIL'S DINERO
by Marshall Grover

Plagued by remorse, a rich old reprobate hired the Texas Troubleshooters to deliver a fortune in greenbacks to each of his victims. Even before Larry and Stretch rode out of Cheyenne, a traitor was selling the secret and the hunt was on.

CAMPAIGNING
by Jim Miller

Ambushed on the Santa Fe trail, Sean Callahan is saved from dying by two Indian strangers. Then the trio is joined by a former slave called Hannibal. But there'll be more lead and arrows flying before the band join the legendary Kit Carson in his campaign against the Comanches.